WEDDING AT POKER FLAT

Wedding at Poker Flat

Lexi Post

Wedding at Poker Flat

Poker Flat Series Book #5

Copyright © 2018 by Lexi Post

This book is a work of fiction. The names, characters, places, and incidents are products of the writer's imagination or have been used fictitiously and are not to be construed as real. Any resemblance to persons, living or dead, actual events, locales or organizations is entirely coincidental.

ALL RIGHTS RESERVED. No part of this book may be used or reproduced in any manner whatsoever without written permission from the author.

For information contact Lexi Post at www.lexipostbooks.com

Cover by Syneca Featherstone

Formatting by Bella Media Management

Cover photo: Killion Group, Inc.

Print ISBN: 978-1-949007-08-4

Excerpt of *Cowboys Never Fold* © 2015 by Lexi Post

Excerpt of *Christmas with Angel* © 2015 by Lexi Post

Wedding At Poker Flat
Poker Flat Series, Book 5

By Lexi Post

Wade Johnson wants to make their wedding perfect for his bride-to-be. The problem is, "perfect" doesn't exist at Poker Flat.

Kendra Lowe, former professional poker player and owner of Poker Flat Nudist Resort, is more than ready to marry her almost perfect cowboy, but when her mother arrives a week early, she's unprepared for the emotions and baggage that come with her—from her mom's blunt ways, to old memories, to her parents' coming divorce.

Wade has finally convinced his fiancé to tie the knot. Unfortunately, there are more knots that need to be untied first. Luckily, the misfit band of employees at Poker Flat are determined to help him get her to the altar…one way or another.

Gun-shy after her first beautiful wedding ended in a demoralizing marriage and harsh divorce, Kendra's hoping this one will be anything but perfect. As hard as it is for her to accept, some things are simply out of her control. It's very clear that this wedding will depend more on her family, friends, and if love truly can conquer all. If it can, it's even stronger than she is.

Acknowledgments

For Bob Fabich, Sr., my very own protector and biggest supporter. And for my sister Paige Wood, whose advice is so important to my books—stories, covers and all.

A huge thank you to Bette Read for the names for Donna's dogs, and to Alison Pridie and Emily Kirkpatrick for naming Donna's husband. Also, thank you to Lisa Fishback for naming Wade's niece.

A special thank you to fellow author and good friend Tiffani Lynn for all her help with my summer of cowboys.

As usual, I owe a lot to my fantastic critique partner, Marie Patrick, whose weekly phones calls always make me smile.

And to my prepub crew, Lisa Fishback, KC Crocker and Carolyn Derrico, a huge thank you for all your help.

AUTHOR'S NOTE

Wedding at Poker Flat was inspired by Bret Harte's short story, *The Outcasts of Poker Flat*, first published in 1869. In Harte's story, four members of Poker Flat society—a gambler, a prostitute, a madam, and a drunk—are banned from the western settlement when a sudden urge to be virtuous overtakes the citizens. On their way to the next settlement, the outcasts stop to rest at the base of the high mountains they will need to cross, but as it's November, it is quite cold. An innocent couple, a young man and his fiancée (a tavern waitress), descends from the mountain tops and rests with them. The young man idolizes the poker player and tells him they are going to Poker Flat to marry. The outcasts recognize the goodness of the two young people and adjust their behavior so as not to taint them. As the odd group converse, a blizzard buries them in snow. In the end, none, outcast nor innocent, survive.

What if the poker player was a woman and the young man a full-grown cowboy and they fell in love and decided to get married? Can the poker player truly leave behind her humble beginnings? Can the cowboy truly love such an unconventional woman? And will their band of outcasts help or hurt? It all depends on how strong love is.

CHAPTER ONE

Wednesday

Kendra Lowe absently reached for her ringing phone. "Yes." Her mind was on the profit and loss statement on her computer screen. Closing Poker Flat for five days for the wedding would hurt their bottom line.

"Sorry to bother you, boss, but I have a woman up here at the garage claiming to be your mother."

"What?" She glanced at the time. It was almost one in the morning.

"I didn't know I'd need a security clearance just to see my own daughter." Her mother's voice came through Mac's phone loud and clear. "Remind her she invited me to her wedding."

"Did you catch that?" Her security guard's tone held quite a bit of sarcasm, and she couldn't blame her.

"Yes, I did. Bring her down. I'll meet you."

"You've got it." Mac ended the call.

She looked at the small calendar on her desk. The wedding

was still over a week away on Thursday. Her mother was supposed to arrive on Monday.

What the hell was she supposed to do with her mother with guests still at Poker Flat?

Quickly, she hit the keyboard and pulled up the reservations. "Well, damn." Scanning the list of rooms on the resort one more time, she closed it out and rose. Out of habit, she unclipped her dark hair, jammed the brown cowboy hat on her head then grabbed up her sweatshirt and strode out of her office, toward the floor-to-ceiling glass double doors of the log and stucco main building.

Solar ground lights lit the desert pathways outside as well as the circular dirt area for golf carts when guests came in for meals or events. The area directly outside was empty, everyone in their casitas or at each other's depending upon their preferences.

Hopefully, none of them would go out for a midnight stroll and drop into the main building like one pair had last night. The last thing she needed was for her mother to stare in horror at a pair of naked guests.

She leaned on one leg and watched the dull yellow lights of a golf cart crest the other side of the ravine and slowly wind down the switchback path that led to a tiny stream at the bottom. It would be a while before they crossed the bridge at the bottom and made it up to the main building.

She hated waking Wade up in the middle of the night, but there was no way around it. At least the new signal booster made it possible to have service now and she *could* call instead of having to drive over. It still didn't reach all of the resort, but enough. She pulled out her phone.

"What's wrong?" His deep voice on the other end settled her nerves far better than any drink could.

Just another reason why she loved him. "Sorry I had to wake you, but my mother just arrived."

"Now? Today?"

She could envision his warm brown eyes widening. "Those were my thoughts exactly, but it's really her. Mac's bringing her to the main building. She's going to have to sleep on our couch tonight."

The momentary silence was telling. "No casita available?"

It wasn't really a question. "No." She didn't want her mother in their space either. It wasn't that she didn't love the woman. She just didn't have a lot of respect for her. She had no backbone. Oh, she talked a good game, but when push came to shove, she always caved.

A heavy sigh sounded over the phone. "I guess there's no help for it. Don't get me wrong, I'm looking forward to meeting her."

She smirked. That was so Wade. "I know you are." He was the one who insisted she invite her mother. Actually, he'd asked her to invite both her parents but she drew the line at her mom. "Too bad we couldn't put her in the massage room, but I'm sure there are early morning appointments."

"And that wouldn't be very comfortable for her."

"What about Jorge's office? That has a nice big comfy couch in there. Far bigger than ours." The lights across the ravine had disappeared, which meant her mother was on her way up. "Do you know if any trail rides are scheduled tomorrow morning?"

"Hold on, let me check." The sound of her fiancé's bare feet on the tile floor came through the phone before he pulled out the chair in their home office. "I thought the plane ticket you sent was for next week."

"It was." Which is why she was more than just a little confused. "I don't think it's even arrived yet." What was she going to do with her mother for a week? Poker Flat was a nudist resort and last she knew, her mother wasn't a nudist. Actually, she sincerely hoped that hadn't changed. That was a sight she really didn't want to—

"We're in luck. No rides tomorrow at all. Looks like the horses have the day off. I'll get dressed and run our extra set of sheets and a blanket over there. If you can grab a pillow from the linen room, she should be set for the night."

And that was another reason she loved him. He was one step ahead of her half the time. "I will. Thank you." She headed back down the hall to the laundry area.

"You know you'll owe me one."

She laughed, knowing exactly what he had in mind. "And I'll be happy to 'pay' up." She grabbed their last new pillow all wrapped in plastic and turned out the light. "I'm looking forward to it. The sooner the better." As she entered the lobby again, a glow of lights appeared near the ridge. "I have to go. She's here."

"Remember." Wade's voice held amusement.

Her heart warmed. "I know. You're all-in. See you soon, Cowboy." She ended the call and put her phone in the back pocket of her jeans before taking a deep breath.

As the golf cart pulled in front of the main doors, she strode forward, her cowboy boots loud in the empty building. Pushing one large glass door open, she smiled. Truth be told, she was excited to see her mother again. It has been a few years.

"There she is. The queen." Donna Lowe grabbed the side of

the golf cart and unfolded herself from the seat with a grunt. "That was a long ass freakin' ride."

Ignoring the usual complaint, Kendra stepped forward. "Hi, mom."

Her mother, who was more than a few inches shorter than her, finally focused on her and gave her a brief hug, her rose perfume filling the air. When she stepped back she squinted. "Did you get taller?"

"No, I'm the same height I was when I saw you last." Her mother's normally white hair was dyed a dark red now, but she had two inches of roots showing on either side of her part. She had it cut like a bob, but it was not well done and needed a good combing. Her eyebrows, which had been drawn on, were crooked and very large, making her look somewhat surprised.

The button-down shirt she wore to cover her own large chest was wrinkled and revealed more cleavage than a woman of her age should, but it was still a step up from her usual clothing. Her striped leggings made her skinny legs look even smaller. With her waist as big as her chest, people who didn't know her might think she would topple over like Humpty-Dumpty.

Her mother wiped her hands on her shirt as if they were sweaty. "I'm shrinking. That's what it is." She turned to Mac, who was seriously tall and fit. Not only that but with her black hair pulled back tight and in her black sweats, she was hard to see at night. "You're gonna bring my sweeties and the rest of my bags now, right?"

Mac shook her head. "Not until Kendra tells us where you're staying. Like I said, the resort is full." Mac moved her gaze to her. "Right, boss?"

She nodded. "We are, but I'm sure mom is tired, so we can put her in Jorge's office for tonight. In the morning, Lacey can work her magic I'm sure."

"Office? What? You expect me to sleep on a desk or something?" Her mother frowned, clearly expecting the worse. "Why can't I stay with you?"

"I'm afraid all I have is a small couch and Jorge's office has a big comfy one. Wade has already gone over there and made it up for you."

Her mother crossed her arms over her ample bosom. "The groom. I want to meet this man. I didn't inspect your last fiancé before that marriage and look how that worked out."

Her chest squeezed at the reminder of what an idiot she'd been. "Very true. I'm sure Wade will answer any questions you have tomorrow. I think we should get you settled in."

"To an office. Nice way to treat your mother."

Kendra ignored her mother's mumbled words. She had no doubt her mom would be thrilled with the accommodations once she saw them. "Mac, why didn't you just bring her bags down on the cart?" She'd noticed there was only one bag on the back.

Mac glanced at her mother. "Because we're going to need the wagon to get them all down here."

"What?" She looked at her mom. "What did you bring? The kitchen sink?"

Her mother's lips formed a slow, smug smile. "I would have if I could have cut the pipes."

Airlines charged per bag. Her mother didn't have that kind of money. In fact, she couldn't have received the airline ticket yet, since it had just been mailed two days ago. "Mom, how did you get here?" Even if she took the bus, a cab ride to Poker Flat would have been over a hundred dollars from the Phoenix station.

Her mother shrugged. "I drove."

She widened her eyes. "Drove? You and Fred bought a second car?" Could the man who produced her have gotten his act together after all these years?

Her mother laughed. "Not even close. I took the car, everything I could fit in it and all the money in our account. I've left your father. I'm going to live here while the divorce goes through. Aren't you happy?"

In complete shock, it took her a moment to notice the vibration in her back pocket. Turning away from her mother's triumphant smile, she answered the phone. "Yes?" Her voice came out in a whisper.

"Kendra, what's wrong?" Wade's voice on the other end had her heart clicking into a more normal rhythm. Only he had the sixth sense when it came to her emotions.

Taking a few steps away from her mom, she kept her voice low. "Mom just informed me she's divorcing Fred and plans to live here until it goes through."

Wade's low whistle on the other end reassured her he understood exactly how impossible the situation was. "That's a big pile of shit to deal with at this early hour in the morning. Just bring her over here, and we'll hash it all out later."

"Right."

"That's awfully rude." Her mother's voice carried as it always did. "It's the middle of the fucking night and she has to take a phone call? I thought this was a nudie resort. Why do you have sweats on?"

Mac's low tones floated over. "Because staff are not allowed to go nude while working."

"That seems weird. You'd think everyone would be nude here."

Kendra took a deep breath. "We'll be right there." Ending the call, she spun around and strode toward her mom. "Okay, let's get you to bed."

"Who was that? Don't they know it's the middle of the night? I've been driving for hours just to see you and you take a call? What's wrong with this generation?"

She ignored her mom's complaining, something she'd learned to do at an early age. "Mac, I'll take it from here. You can grab another golf cart."

"Will do." Her crazy-fit female security guard wasted no time jumping onto another golf cart and beating a hasty exit. Kendra didn't blame her.

Finally, she turned back to her mom. "If you'd like to climb back in, I'll take you over to the stable manager's office. It's a whole separate building and has everything you'll need including a full bathroom."

Her mother stepped up into the passenger side of the cart still grumbling. "Now you're putting me in a stable. What do I look like, Mary Magdalene? I'm not pregnant. I'm not fat either. Things just shifted. It's called post menopause and it will happen to you, too. Just wait. Hey, what about my stuff? Is that amazon going to bring them?"

She turned the cart on and pressed the pedal. "Not tonight. I want to get you a real room, so you can have your own space. There are no trail rides scheduled tomorrow, but I'm sure Jorge and Crystal will need to use the office at some point."

Her mother grabbed a hold of the side of the cart as they went over a rock. "So now I'm an inconvenience?"

"Of course not. We just weren't expecting you until next week. Every guest room is booked right now. It's winter and high season for tourists." She glanced at her mom. "I wanted to make as much money as possible so I can afford to feed all our wedding guests." That her mother would get.

"That's my girl. You take after me, you know. Your father couldn't keep a nickel in his pocket if it was stuck in there with chewed gum. But me—" Her mother's smile became devious. "I know how to stretch a penny and save. What your father doesn't know won't hurt him."

Her stomach lurched. She didn't want to know, but her gut told her she would soon be learning all the torrid details. She was torn about her mother's announcement. Half of her was damn proud of her. Fred had always treated her mother like crap. She'd even stopped calling him dad at the age of nine because she couldn't stand the thought that they were related in any way.

But the other half of her worried about the repercussions of her mother's decision, both in what might happen for her mom and how it would affect her and Wade. Fred wouldn't take his housekeeper and cook skipping out on him laying down.

She drove the golf cart up the slight incline toward the barn and office. Despite knowing she'd probably regret it, she had to ask. "Why did you finally leave Fred? He didn't hurt you, did he?" The thought of him hitting her mother had her hands squeezing the steering wheel.

"Of course not! If he dared lay a hand on me, I'd beat his flabby ass from here to kingdom come."

She relaxed. Fred was an unfaithful asshole and a drunk, but he'd never done anything physically abusive. He didn't have to, his mouth did it all for him.

"Then why did you leave him now?"

Her mother grinned. "When you called and said you owned a resort and were getting married, I figured you had finally settled down."

Okay, that might be true, but what did that have to do with leaving Fred? "I don't understand."

"It's simple. Sally left the park after her husband died and moved in with her son and daughter-in-law. Betty's daughter renovated her garage into a mother-in-law apartment so Betty could leave that falling apart trailer she was living in. And now I can move here to be with my daughter."

Kendra was back to squeezing the steering wheel as she pulled to a stop in front of the stable manager's office next to the golf cart already parked there, her shock and fear so complete she wasn't sure she could move.

Luckily, Wade opened the door and strode out. Her broad-shouldered, thin waisted cowboy had a smile on his face as he walked toward her mother's side of the golf cart. "You must be Donna. I'd know you were Kendra's mother even in a crowded fair. You're obviously where she got her good looks."

Her mother looked at her and rolled her eyes before turning back to Wade. "Well now, if that ain't a crock of shit I don't know what is." She waved him toward her. "And you just keep piling it on, honey."

Wade chuckled as he tipped his hat, barely revealing his short chocolate-brown hair beneath. "I'll do my best, ma'am."

Her mother looked over at her again. "Is he for real?"

She managed a weak nod.

"Well, damn me to hell and back. I'm gonna like it here." Her mother turned toward Wade, who offered her his hand to help her out. "Oh, yes, I'm going to like it here a lot."

As Wade guided her mother into the office, she forced her fingers to let go of the steering wheel. Already her mind was racing with one disastrous scenario after the other. Her mother insulting a guest. Her mother getting drunk at the bar. Her mother spinning out on a golf cart and it toppling over. Her mother walking into her house when she and Wade were having sex. Her mother stalking into the kitchen to complain to Selma about her meal.

She lowered her head onto the steering wheel and closed her eyes. Maybe if she wished hard enough, she'd discover this was all just a bad dream.

"Hey." She looked up to find Mac standing next to the golf cart.

She scanned the area but didn't see another cart nearby. The woman was as quiet as Hunter, her other security guard, and both of them did a fantastic job. Would they be willing to escort her mother off the property? She shook her head. That wasn't an option. Nothing was an option, and that scared the hell out of her.

"Anything I can do?"

She shook her head. "No. Not yet anyway. She just informed me she plans to live here. Indefinitely."

Even in the low illumination of the single spotlight on the outside of the barn, Mac's shiver was clear. "That will be… interesting."

"Hah." The understatement was laughable. "Far worse than

that." She pulled herself together and exited the cart. "Did you need something?"

Mac's mouth formed a grin. "Yes, I was wondering what you wanted me to do with the dogs."

"What dogs?" She scanned the dirt area in front of the barn, but didn't see any dogs. She didn't even hear a coyote, which was odd.

"Her dogs." Mac pointed toward the office. "They're in her car. I didn't realize they were there because they were so quiet, but I was just up there and they must have woken up because they are yapping like crazy."

Dogs? Her mother didn't have any dogs. Last she knew her mother didn't like dogs. For that matter neither did she. They were too much like coyotes for her comfort. As if her childhood trauma had happened yesterday, her left leg started to itch. She really didn't like dogs. "Are they big?"

Mac shook her head. "I've owned cats bigger than these dogs."

Her tension eased. That was the first good news she'd had all night, which in itself was pretty sad. "You better bring them down here. Put them in the unfinished Saloon."

"I'll check and bring anything in the vehicle that might help. She was adamant about locking her car, but then she handed me the key to bring down her bags."

Kendra waved the idiosyncrasy off. "That's typical. I'll have Wade and Jorge get the rest of her things once I find out from Lacey where and when we can move her."

"Got it. I'll be back."

Mac strode off, disappearing into the desert beyond the circle of light. She knew far more about Mac than anyone on the resort and she was proud at how the woman had fit in. She'd kept more than her fair share of vandals off the property. That and the teenagers with more curiosity than brains.

Squaring her shoulders, she moved toward the office. If she left Wade alone in there with her mother any longer, he might think twice about marrying her. Even at the thought, her gut twisted. Here she was the one who had delayed the wedding plans and now she wished they'd eloped before he ever met her family.

Luckily, there was just the one. Fred was not family.

Wade barely kept himself from laughing out loud as they exited the office and he guided Kendra to his golf cart. Her mother both shocked and amused him, mainly because she was the complete opposite of her daughter.

Kendra sat in the passenger seat and opened her mouth to speak.

He put a finger over her lips and shook his head.

After she nodded in understanding, he walked around to the driver seat and sat next to her, turning the cart on and driving back to their house, the only two-story adobe place on the resort. Once they had passed the Old West town, the newest addition to the resort, he glanced at her. "Go ahead. Spill."

She frowned, which was far better than how she used to register her frustration, which had been showing no emotion at all. Still, he knew the frown was just the tip of the iceberg with his soon to be wife.

"She wants to live here. Did you hear that? On a nudist resort. The wedding isn't for another week and she's already moving in. And what the hell are we going to do with her until then? I can just see her making fun of a man's penis and the next thing you know, we'll be all over the nudist internet as the place to avoid. I didn't build this place just so she could kill it."

Kendra took a breath, so he jumped in. "I'm sure she doesn't want to ruin your livelihood. You're her daughter."

"You don't understand." She shook her head. "I'm not saying she will purposefully ruin me. You heard her in there? She doesn't have a clue what she's saying."

He chuckled. "You mean about how she understands now why you went for such a big piece of meat?"

Kendra groaned. "Everyone except you would be pissed off by that. I can just imagine what she'll say when she—Oh, hell."

"What?" Even in the dark, he could see the mortification in Kendra's face as she looked at him.

"Your parents. She's going to totally embarrass me."

He brought the golf cart to a stop in front of their door, then took her by the shoulders and turned her to face him. "They'll love her because she's your mother."

She shook her head. "Now you're outright lying to me. I've met your parents. They are polite and caring and…and…nice. They'll spend three minutes with her and run the other way."

"Kendra, listen to me. My parents won't break because your mother says things most people don't. My grandmother is like that, and we all do just fine."

Her eyes rounded. "Freak. Tomorrow's the manager's reception. What are we going to do with her while we're hosting our guests? There's no way I'll let her see me nude."

Obviously, his fiancé was going off the deep-end fast and that actually scared him. She'd faced an opinionated sheriff bent on destroying her dream with more backbone than this. "Kendra, listen to me."

She looked at him but she wasn't seeing him.

Screw that. Grasping her by the neck, he pulled her to him and kissed her. It only took a second before she responded. As their tongues entwined he held her until her hands started to burrow under his shirt.

As much as he wanted to make love to her, they weren't doing it outside on the golf cart and they weren't doing it until he got through to her. Breaking the kiss, he leaned his forehead against hers. "Let's go inside and talk about this calmly, okay?"

She nodded, her breaths already short from her desire.

"Good." He let her go and met her in front of the cart, taking her hand as they walked to the door.

Chapter Two

Wednesday continued.

Kendra remained silent until they entered, then she plopped down on the couch and stared at the coffee table. "Maybe I can get Lacey to take mom to Last Chance for a few days."

Wade moved into the kitchen and turned on the coffeemaker manually since it wasn't due to start for another couple of hours. Then opening the refrigerator, he twisted open a beer and brought it to Kendra. "Here, it will help you think."

She glanced up at him. "I'd rather it help me forget."

He shook his head and sat next to her, putting his arm around her shoulders. "The problem would still be there. Now let's take this one step at a time. First, the manager's reception tomorrow."

She groaned even as she lifted the beer bottle to her lips.

He forced himself to look away from her mouth, lowering his gaze which gave him a perfect view of her bountiful cleavage. She continued to dress to cover her large chest and her scarred left leg though she stripped for the Manager's Reception on Wednesdays.

At that realization, he leaned back. She still wasn't comfortable with who she was. He took a minute to digest that. Kendra was one of the most confident women he'd ever met. She'd made it through her first marriage despite the man's callous attitude, become a very successful professional poker player, and created a haven for nudists who wanted a top-notch resort for vacations despite all the hurdles thrown in her way.

Yet for all that, she was still insecure about two things, her body and her upbringing in a trailer park. He'd been trying to help with the first insecurity, but had missed the second. As husband material, that was a significant strike against him.

"So, do you have any solutions?"

Her voice had him returning his attention to the problem at hand. "I do. One of us can go and one of us can distract your mother. Maybe take her into town for dinner."

She nodded. "That'll work. I'll let Buddy and Ginger know mom is here so they don't make a big deal over one of us not being at the reception." She rose and walked toward the kitchen, the smell of coffee starting to drift in. "I have no idea how mom is going to react to seeing Buddy and Ginger here." She opened a cupboard and pulled out a coffee mug.

He stifled the urge to smile. His soon-to-be wife was usually sound asleep when he woke up in the morning, so the fact she thought to pour him his coffee had his heart warming. "You didn't tell her when you spoke to her on the phone?"

She leaned against the island that separated the kitchen from the living room, her weight thrown over to her right hip, a clear indication she was agitated. "No. I had planned to tell her on the drive from the airport to here. I thought it would give me enough time to answer any objections."

"Objections?"

"Yes. Mom was one of those who was happy to get rid of the 'nudie people' when that all went down at the trailer park. But when she found out I had opened a nudist resort, she only asked if it was making money and if I had a section for trailers. That made me think that maybe mom was glad to see Ginger and Buddy thrown out because she resented me spending time with them when I was young. Either way, I have no idea how she feels now."

The coffee maker beeped and Kendra turned away.

He enjoyed the sight of her in the kitchen as she lifted the pot. He'd never thought that he'd be living on a nudist resort with a woman who didn't rise at the crack of dawn with him. He owed a lot to his friend Dale for asking him to work at Poker Flat for three months. If it hadn't been for him, he would have missed out on an amazing woman and a unique community that took him in with open arms.

She brought him the coffee and handed it to him.

"Thank you. You could tell your mother at dinner and I can host the reception." It wasn't as if he had to do anything besides welcome everyone and talk. Lacey and Selma had the weekly event going off like clockwork.

"That could work." She returned to stand by the counter, her former outburst forgotten as she buried it under her poker façade.

That used to bother him, but he understood her now. It was a defense mechanism. He didn't mind because he had many ways of getting her out of her closed place. Taking a sip of coffee, he barely kept from closing his eyes in satisfaction. He was an early riser, but not this early. "And today, I'll have Jorge take your mom for a trail ride."

As he expected, Kendra's eyes widened. "A trail ride? My mother? I'm not sure she's even seen a real live horse before, never mind ridden one."

He shrugged. "If Jorge can't convince her to try horseback riding, I'm sure he could get her on the wagon at least to a spot where they could walk to. Maybe Selma could pack them a picnic lunch."

"I'm not sure."

"Why?" He took another sip of coffee. He saw nothing wrong with his plan.

Kendra pulled away from the counter to walk across the living room then sat beside him. "I think Selma likes Jorge."

"What?" He hadn't seen that coming. Sure, Jorge flirted with the older woman, but he flirted with every woman. The man made very good tips.

"It's just a hunch, but she complains so much about him, I think she likes him."

That made absolutely no sense, so he let it go. "Tell you what. I'll ask him anyway. If Selma does like him, we'll know right away."

"I'll say." Her lip finally quirked up into a small smile. "You'll have to tell me exactly how she reacts. If I was betting, I'd lay money down that she likes the man."

He wiggled his eyebrows. "Did you want to make a bet on it?"

Her blue eyes sparkled with mischief. "That depends on what the stakes are. It's not like I haven't seen you naked already, so that's no incentive."

Her reminder of the first time they played poker —strip poker—made him pause. He took another sip of coffee, the caffeine helping him to think. She was very good at reading people. She'd done it for a living. If she was right, and as surprising as it might be that the two fifty-somethings might be interested in each other, he needed to make the win worth it for Kendra.

She raised her eyebrows at him. "Well?"

"What would you want?"

Her smiled turned devious, which immediately heated his blood. "If I'm right, I choose where we go for our honeymoon."

He froze, his coffee cup halfway to the end table. "I thought you said we couldn't take a honeymoon because it's the busy season." He'd been irritated that she'd put the business before them, but had sucked it up. Just getting her to commit to a wedding date had been a major win for him. He'd never expected to be the one itching to get married.

"Oh, I don't mean right now. But I thought about what you said last year and you're right. We do deserve a honeymoon. We hardly get anytime to ourselves living here on the resort. So I was thinking maybe we could go this summer. Things will be slower and the staff should be able to handle it, or we could simply close for a couple weeks and give everyone paid time off."

He finished setting his cup down. She surprised him on a daily basis with the way her mind worked and with the size of her heart. He'd take the bet just to get her to commit to the honeymoon alone. "And if I win, I choose the spot?"

She shrugged. "Sure."

Her utter confidence had him holding back a smile. Most likely she was right about Selma, but he knew his fiancé. If she had to work at something, it made her even more determined. "Deal."

"Good." She gave him a nod, but he recognized the loosening of her shoulders.

Something told him she had a place in mind that he may not like. He hoped he was wrong.

"So that covers distracting mom today and tonight. At least that gives me time to figure out what to do with her for the following four days." Even as she said it, Kendra leaned her head back against the couch and closed her eyes.

It was now just past four in the morning, a time neither of them was usually awake. Moving off the couch, he knelt on the throw rug and lifted her foot. Taking off first one cowboy boot and then the other, he smiled sadly at the memory of the first time he'd seen her scarred leg. It had taken months, but she didn't flinch anymore when he touched her there.

"Wade, you don't have to do that."

He looked up at her, but she hadn't opened her eyes. "I know." He set the boots aside before taking off her socks. He gently massaged her feet, wishing he could take her worry about her mother completely off her shoulders.

"Hmm, that feels so good."

At her words, an idea struck. It might only take her mind off her mom for a short period of time, but it would definitely relax her. Her problem was she took responsibility for everything, rarely admitting that anything was beyond her control. He knew one sure way to topple that in her psyche.

He ran his hand up her legs to the top of her jeans and unbuttoned them.

As his fingers found the zipper, her hand covered his. "What are you doing?"

He glanced up to see her eyes were still closed, her head still back against the couch.

"I'm undressing you. You've had a long day."

"Uh-hmm."

At her agreement, he swept aside her hand and unzipped her jeans. Hooking his fingers inside the waistband of both her pants and her panties, he worked them down. "Lift."

Her hips rose until he worked the material past her ass, then she dropped them back onto the couch cushion. That she hadn't argued with him was telling. She wasn't just tired physically, but mentally.

Pulling her jeans off, he pushed back the throw rug as he moved the coffee table out of the way. To avoid cluing her in, he knelt before her again, ignoring the erection growing in his jeans to unbutton her tan western shirt and flick open the front clasp of her bra.

Her large breasts pushed the cups aside as if they'd been anxious to come out. She sighed, but didn't move.

Quietly, he unbuttoned his own jeans and slid the zipper down, giving him some breathing room. With that accomplished, he began to work her shirt over her shoulders. Pulling her willing body toward him, he pushed the shirt down her arms until both sleeves were half off.

Slowly, he brought the ends of the sleeves together behind her back and tied them.

Her breath caught. "Wade." Though her tone was a warning, the hoarseness of her voice revealed her true feelings.

He didn't respond. Instead, he looped the sleeve ends one more time to knot them. When he leaned her back against the couch her arms behind her, he found her eyes open and darkened with desire. Yet still, she shook her head. "We can't. You have to—"

He pressed two fingers against her lips. "I have to take my woman."

Her chest rose as she took a deep breath.

He'd used the word *take* on purpose. They made love in many ways, sometimes quick, sometimes gentle, sometimes slowly, but he'd discovered only by taking total control of her could he help her when she felt overwhelmed. "No more words."

Her eyelids grew heavy as he spoke. That she responded so quickly proved how much she needed this.

Moving his two fingers over her chin and down her neck, he felt her swallow. He wanted to kiss that very spot, but he resisted and continued lower, straight down between her breasts. Her rosy nipples were already hard and begging for attention, and they would receive it in due time.

He trailed his fingers lower, over her tight abs to her belly button. Again, he resisted the urge to stop and play and continued down her smooth skin, over her abdomen and down to her mons.

Kendra opened her legs, giving him access to whatever he wished.

Slowing his hand, he felt the hard nub of her clit beneath the pads of his two fingers and stopped.

His own desire inhibited his breathing, forcing him to take in more air to keep his focus. Gently, he let his fingers rest against her, pressing on her slightly.

Her legs spread wider, but she made no sound.

She wanted him to continue his journey and find her opening, but making her wait, not get what she wanted when she wanted it, was all part of freeing her from her burdens. He couldn't let her direct his movements.

He dropped his other hand onto her knee, the surprise touch causing her to start. Good. He didn't want her to guess his intention. He removed his hand and set it on her waist. Again, her breathing hitched.

Smiling, he lifted his hand and rested it on her shoulder. This time she relaxed. So he lifted it again and cupped her left breast. Beneath his hand, he felt the speed of her heartrate increase.

She'd finally fully capitulated, given up all control, which meant their lovemaking would refresh her in more ways than one.

What she didn't know was what that did to him. It was all he could do not to flip her on to the floor and take her. He tried to think of it as good willpower practice, but his cock could care less.

Refocusing his thoughts on the soft mass cupped in his hand, he squeezed it, gently massaging the globe, but staying away from the pebbled skin of her areola. Without giving her a clue, he leaned forward and bared his teeth.

With well-practiced precision, he nipped at the hard nipple above his palm.

She moaned, but didn't push her breast into his face like she normally would have.

To reward her for her capitulation, he took the hard nub between his teeth again and rolled it back and forth.

Her head lolled to the side as her breathing grew short.

With no warning, he pulled the nipple into his mouth and sucked hard.

Her moan this time was louder and her hips bucked against his fingers, pressing her clit between them.

He immediately let go of her breast. "I will decide what pleasure to give you and when."

She nodded. It wasn't the first time they'd done this. She well understood how her orgasm would be if she let him control everything.

He grinned despite his discomfort. She wasn't very good at waiting…usually. To reward her for her patience, he moved his fingers twice in a circle against her clit, watching her as her mouth opened with her pleasure.

Though he told her he loved her, she didn't fully comprehend how deep his feelings went. Despite that, he had no doubt she loved him. There was no half anything with her.

Leaning toward her again, he distracted her by brushing her left nipple with his thumb. Then he licked at her right nipple before gently sucking it in to his mouth, while his tongue continued to play.

He craved the taste of her and as soon as his brain registered that she'd remain pliant beneath him. Giving in, he sucked hard, his finger pinching her other nipple.

Her groan was an aphrodisiac that was too hard to resist. He moved his fingers on her clit up and down, keeping the pressure light, while her breasts received harder attention.

Stopping to view the rosy nipples and allow the sensations to subside, he caught his own control before returning to her pleasure, his fingers against her clit, never stopping.

The scent of her readiness filled his nostrils while his mouth and fingers were busy, making his movement jerks, instead of smooth. He couldn't allow that and immediately lightened up on her body, keeping his strokes light, despite his rock-hard cock.

Taking his hand from her breast, he pulled his cock from his jeans, ignoring the light scrape of the zipper, which helped him find some semblance of control. It wasn't much, but it would have to do.

Opening his mouth, he released her breast and straightened to gaze at her flushed face. The soft, low sounds coming from her filled his heart with love. Sitting back on his heels, he removed his fingers from her clit and used his hands to spread her legs wider.

The hitch in Kendra's breath was the only reaction she gave.

He couldn't resist the scent of her desire any longer. Keeping one hand on her thigh, he lowered his head.

At the touch of Wade's tongue on her opening, Kendra's sheath tightened of its own accord. Luckily, Wade couldn't know that or he might stop. It took all her will to remain relaxed and accepting. What awaited her if she did, was an intense orgasm that she could lose herself in.

He stroked upward and over her clit, as he gripped her legs to hold her in place. His tongue made another swipe, this time playing with her hard nub, eliciting sharp slices of pleasure before delving into her sheath.

He was magic with his tongue, repeating the same pattern multiple times, increasing her need until she started to pant. Then he let up, barely flicking at her clit only to blow air on it.

As he began to play again, increasing his pressure, his fingers found her right nipple and rolled it. The excitement was so strong that she had to hiss to keep from bucking her hips upward. If she did, he'd lighten his ministrations.

He must have been pleased with her reaction, because his tongue didn't leave her clit and the movements grew stronger. When his other hand left her leg, she hoped his finger would move inside her, but it didn't. Instead, he captured her other nipple, giving it the same pinching pressure and roll as the first.

Her sheath was filled with readiness, but the illusive orgasm remained out of reach, Wade's continued touching neither increasing or decreasing. She moaned, almost crying out with her desire, not sure she could wait, but even as she thought to force it by touching herself, the bonds of her shirt sleeves kept her from interfering.

He must have sensed her exquisite torture because his tongue suddenly stopped and was replaced with his lips. He gently sucked her clit between his teeth.

Her orgasm swept through her like a dust storm, obliterating all thought and sweeping her up to the pinnacle of ecstasy. She whimpered as she was tossed about by the sharp highs and lows of ultimate pleasure. Just as her world began to right itself, Wade pulled her forward and laid her out on the cold tile floor. As her nipples made contact with the hard surface, they hardened again, and she shuddered with anticipation.

Her hands, still tied behind her back, her face on the floor, she was at his mercy. Wade's low growl behind her keyed her senses that he wouldn't wait to take her. As soon as his hands pulled her ass up, she knew it would be hard and fast. Her sheath flooded with that knowledge just before his cock thrust inside her to the hilt.

His hands came down on either side of her, and he pulled

out only to push in so hard that she slid a few inches on the floor. As if that was exactly what he wanted, he did it again, her nipples coming in contact with the rough grout between the tiles. The added friction tightened her sheath.

He thrust again, moving her across the floor a few inches at a time, her hands helpless to stop it as another dip between the tiles hit. This time when he pulled back, he grabbed her tied arms with his teeth and brought her back with him.

Her clit scraped, her nipples scraped, and his next thrust threw her over the edge. Her orgasm gripped her as Wade continued to thrust, finally kneeling back and pulling her hips back with him to spend himself inside her, prolonging her pleasure as he filled her.

When they'd regained more even breathing, he untied her hands, and pulled her up, holding her tight against his naked chest, his face against her back. She smiled that he'd managed to whip off his shirt but not his pants.

She leaned forward and he released her. Pulling herself off him, she turned around and sat on the floor to face him. "Thank you."

He looped his hand around her neck and pulled her in for a long, lingering kiss. When he was done tasting her, he leaned his forehead against her. "My pleasure."

She chuckled. "No, really. It was all mine.

CHAPTER THREE

Wednesday continued.

Wade drove the golf cart just a little faster than appropriate. He hadn't wanted to leave Kendra until she'd fallen asleep, but that had put him behind. He smiled as he passed the old west town across from the corral and barn. He wouldn't be surprised if she was late to work, too.

At the ring on his phone, he let up on the acceleration and let the cart roll to a stop as he answered. "Hey, Mac."

"I need a little help here. I've got a man with a rattlesnake bite and a hysterical wife."

He glanced at the Stable Manager's office, relieved to see no golf cart there signaling either Jorge or Crystal had arrived yet. "Are you at the main building?"

"Yes. I've called for an ambulance, but nothing I say is getting through to her."

He hit the accelerator and turned the wheel. "I'm on my way." Ending the call, he headed away from both the residences and the barn, taking the pathway down the forked dip and up to the main building faster than he should. If Kendra saw the dust cloud he left, her good mood would evaporate.

As he crested the small hill to the dirt parking area for carts in front of the main building, he slowed. Mac looked like a carved statue for all the emotion she revealed as a nude Mrs. Ditzman clearly railed at her.

Pulling up next to the golf cart with Mr. Ditzman, he stepped out.

"Oh, Wade. There's got to be something you can do. He's dying." The woman, maybe fifteen years his senior, and far more wealthy, looked truly panicked. They were from Wisconsin and this was their first visit to Arizona.

A stern tone was definitely in order to cut through her hysteria. He nodded toward Mr. Ditzman, who sat in the cart, not moving at all, his jaw tight. "When did he get bit?"

As he expected, Mrs. Ditzman responded to his authority. "An hour ago." She threw Mac a glare. "Maybe two. I'm not sure. It took forever for her to come."

He glanced over the short woman's head to catch Mac shaking her head. "And where did this occur?"

"We woke up before the sun and decided to go for a walk."

At least it wasn't a rattler in the casita. "So you ignored our warning about walking in the desert while it's dark."

The woman's eyes widened. "How can you talk to me about this when my husband is dying?" Her voice ended on a sob.

Having established that the resort was not responsible, he took pity on her. "Mrs. Ditzman, your husband isn't dying. I promise you."

"How can you say that? Rattlesnakes are poisonous. He's going to die. We have to get to the entrance. The ambulance might be there already. If we're not there, they might leave. Oh, my God, what if they are there now and—"

"The ambulance won't leave. And I can tell you your husband isn't going to die before he reaches the hospital. I know because I've been bitten three times."

That stopped the woman in her tracks. "You have? By a rattlesnake?"

"Yes. It comes with ranching in the desert. They live here, too, so it's not uncommon. Now, do you want to help your husband?"

She nodded, obviously still stupefied by the fact he'd been bitten and had lived to tell the tale.

"Good. Then go back to your casita, get dressed and get some clothes for your husband. The ambulance won't mind transporting him to the hospital naked, but he'll need to leave the hospital eventually. And if you want to go with him, I guarantee they won't let you unless you're dressed.

The woman looked down at herself as if she'd completely forgotten.

"And while you do that, I'll take a look at your husband's snake bite."

Relief swept over the woman's features. "I'll do that, but don't let him leave without me."

"I promise."

Studying him for another second, she finally turned and headed down the path toward the casita they were staying in, but not before throwing Mac a glare.

He strode to their security guard. "Why don't you go home?"

He glanced up at the light hitting the top of the ravine Poker Flat was built in. "It'll be dawn soon anyway."

Mac shook her head. "No, I'm going to head up to the garage and meet the ambulance. I think it only fair to give them a heads-up about Mrs. Ditzman."

He'd been stupidly old-fashioned when Kendra had hired a woman for a security guard, but Mac had earned his respect too many times to count since she'd come on board. "Thanks. I think they'd appreciate that."

Mac didn't say anything else. She just headed out at a jog since Mr. Ditzman was in her golf cart.

Wade turned back and walked up to the golf cart. "How are you feeling, Mr. Ditzman?"

"Like my foot is on fire."

He crouched down to look at the man's foot. Since there was some blood, he wouldn't wrap it. Blood could help the hospital identify the right anti-venom faster. It didn't look like a deep bite, which was good as well. He looked up to assure the man and noticed he was sweating despite the cool temperatures, which meant it was due to the poison. "Mr. Ditzman, you're a lucky man."

"I am? I don't feel lucky right now."

Wade stood. "You are. You have a shallow bite. That means that as long as you remain calm, you will be as good a new in no time. You're also lucky because our hospitals here know a lot about snake bites. And most importantly, you have a wife who loves you very much."

Mr. Ditzman's eyes rounded in surprise, before a small smile lifted the corners of his mouth. "Yeah. She can be a pain, but she does love me."

He looked over the cart to find Mrs. Ditzman hurrying up the path with a bag over her shoulder. She wore two difference sandals, but he didn't say anything. "Why don't you hop on the back there and we'll get you to the ambulance.

Still out of breath from the quick climb, she plopped down on the back seat.

He got behind the wheel and drove as quick as he could down the path, not wanting to jar the man too much. Once they made it to the garage, they found the ambulance just pulling to a stop.

Two paramedics jumped out. He quickly explained what he'd been told and they ushered the couple into the vehicle. Before they shut the door, he stepped to the back. "Mrs. Ditzman, whenever they release your husband, you just call us and we'll send someone over to pick you up and bring you back here.

"Thank you." The woman started to cry then and the doors slammed shut.

He stood next to Mac, watching the ambulance race off. He had no doubt the man would be fine. The wife, however, was a different matter. He thanked fate again for finding Kendra for him. The last thing she'd do is become hysterical during an emergency. Angry maybe, but not hysterical. She'd save her break down for after everything was fine. He grinned at the thought.

"Don't ask me."

Having forgotten Mac was there, he looked at her. "Don't ask you what?"

"Don't ask me to go pick them up. That woman is pathetic." Shaking her head, she started to walk toward the ravine's cliff edge.

"Hey, Mac. Don't you want a ride?" He pointed to the golf cart.

"No." And with that she disappeared over the edge.

Shrugging, he turned toward the cart just as the sun's rays burst over the desert floor, lighting up the landscape and throwing saguaro and mesquite shadows everywhere.

"Shit." He jumped into the golf cart. Jorge would be showing up for work any time now.

He sped down the hairpin dirt road toward the bridge that crossed the small creek, the only part left of the raging river that had once formed the ravine. Once across it, he headed up the other side. He was almost to the top when his phone rang.

"*Putos pendejos! Manténganse fuera de mi cocina. ¿Qué demonios se supone que debo hacer ahora?*"

Pulling the phone from against his ear, he cringed. Selma wasn't happy and if that was the case, that could mean unhappy guests. Without even glancing at the barn, he turned toward the main building. The last thing they needed during high season was an unhappy cook.

Jumping from the cart, he strode to the large double glass doors and yanked one open. His boot heels on the tile floor were loud in the silence of the lobby. As he turned into the dining room, loud swearing came from the kitchen, so he took the most direct line between the tables to push open the batwing doors of Selma's domain.

The woman was still yelling into her phone, her other arm waving as she stood in front of the industrial fridge.

"Selma!"

At his voice, the cook pulled the phone from her ear and looked at it.

"Selma, I'm here. What's the problem?"

She whipped her head around to scowl at him. "*Algún idiota tomó mi crema. No puedo—*"

"Stop, stop. English por favor. My Spanish isn't that good."

"Someone took my cream!" She pointed at the open refrigerator. "I can't make my cinnamon French toast without it. *Dios mio*, what the fuck do I have to do to keep people out of my kitchen at night? Padlock my refrigerators? *Que chupe mi concha.*"

Since her voice rose to a squealing pitch at the end of her question, he didn't think it prudent to point out that Kendra actually owned the appliances. "Let me see what I can do." He used his most calm voice. "You start on whatever you were going to serve with the French toast and I will find your cream. How much will you need?"

Luckily, she'd always had a soft spot for him, though why, he didn't know. At his questions, she started to figure in her head. Finally, she nodded. "Sixteen cups."

He swallowed. A gallon of cream? No wonder her French toast was so good. "And were you serving anything with it?"

Her hands found her hips as she shook her head at him. "Of course. Sausage, bacon, Southwestern scrambled eggs, fresh fruit, warm syrup, and orange juice."

Hell, his mouth watered at the list. "You get started on the other items and I'll get you that cream."

She stared at him for a moment, obviously trying to decide if he would deliver. Finally, she nodded once, then started pulling ingredients from the refrigerator.

Quickly, he exited Selma's domain and headed for the front lobby, pulling his phone from his pocket as he did so. Who the hell would take a gallon of cream? Dialing, he glanced at the clock behind the reception desk. "Shit." Jorge had probably already discovered Mrs. Lowe in his office. Maybe he'd catch a break and Crystal would get to work first.

Striding toward the large glass doors, he paused as the call connected.

"Good morning, Wade." From the sound of Lacey's cheerful voice, she was in her car.

"I need you to pick up a gallon of cream." That was a bit abrupt.

"I just drove out of town." The cheerfulness was gone.

He pushed open the doors and headed for his golf cart. "It's a Selma emergency or I wouldn't be calling."

"Oh, my. No problem. I'll turn around. Is it for breakfast?"

"Yeah." He sat in the cart and turned the key.

"Wait, I just ordered a gallon of cream. It should be in the refrigerator. Didn't she find it?"

He sighed. "She did, but someone took it."

"Well, sugar. I'll be there as fast as I can."

"Thanks." He ended the call and started the cart in motion. If his phone rang one more time, he'd simply chuck it into the ravine. As he crested the small hill to the other side of the split resort, his heart sank. There were two golf carts parked outside the stable manager's office.

No use worrying about what might have happened. He'd just have to clean up whatever mess there was before Kendra came into work. Slowing the cart, he brought it to a stop and got out.

Expecting the worst, he forced himself to open the door with a smile. He lost his smile at the emptiness of the room. "Hello?" He looked at the now empty couch, the sheets and blankets folded and piled on one side. Mrs. Lowe's suitcase sat next to it, so she must still be around somewhere.

At the sound of the toilet flushing down the hall, he relaxed. She must be in the bathroom. Maybe Jorge and Crystal went straight to the barn to feed the horses. He leaned his ass against the desk and waited.

Within minutes, the sound of footsteps that sounded like cowboy boots came down the short hall and Crystal Henderson appeared. She'd been recruited by Hunter, an old friend who needed a second chance. She was their relatively new stable hand and when she saw him her light brown eyes widened. "Good morning, Wade. Were you looking for your future mother-in-law?" She smiled as she pushed her shoulder-length, golden blonde hair back into a ponytail and pulled it through a hair tie.

"Yes, I was. I'm sorry I didn't get here sooner."

She laughed. "Oh, don't be. By time I got here, those two were already best friends and heading out."

"Out? What two?" He was obviously missing something.

"Jorge and Donna. Not that she paid me much attention when the boss introduced me. They went out for a ride. Jorge had brought in some churros he'd conned Selma into giving him last night so we could have a treat this morning, but I'm obviously not getting any. He said Donna could have some at the first crest of the trail when she'd be able to look back and see what a beautiful place her daughter had built."

For some reason the scene that came to mind didn't please him as much as it should. Wasn't that exactly what he'd planned to suggest?

Crystal walked past him and picked up a straw cowboy hat from the desk. "What are you scowling for?"

Scowling? He shook his head. "I'm not sure I'm completely on board with Mrs. Lowe alone with Jorge." At least, not now.

Crystal waved his concern away with a flick of her hand. "Oh, don't worry about them. Jorge may be a charmer, but he totally respects women. Don't forget, he has a daughter. Donna is probably safer with him than she wants to be."

"What?"

She laughed. "Oh, you should have seen that woman checking out his butt when he bent over to pick up the brush she dropped. I'd swear she did it on purpose if she hadn't been so surprised when he got it for her." Crystal grinned as she headed for the door. "Honestly, I hope I'm just like her when I get to be her age." With that final statement, she walked out, leaving him in the silence of the large room.

This could be more of a mess than he anticipated.

The door opened again and Crystal popped her head in. "I almost forgot. Donna said her dogs will need to go out this morning."

He opened his mouth, but the door closed. Dogs? What dogs? Kendra didn't mention any dogs. Or did her mom mean it as an old-fashioned expression for someone's feet. He'd heard his grandmother complain her dogs were tired when she'd been shopping with his mother. And Mrs. Lowe had driven in her car for days so she probably meant she needed to get off her butt. Crystal had probably never heard the expression.

Catching the time on the clock on the wall, he quickly left the office. It had been his office when he'd first come to work for Poker Flat Nudist Resort, but now he and Kendra shared hers, just like they shared her house and soon their lives.

He jumped into the golf cart, but didn't speed as he made his way over to the main building. Guests and employees would be about now and he had to set an example.

That he wasn't completely comfortable with the fact he wasn't bringing much to the marriage besides himself, his family and his bank account weighed on his mind. Then again, Kendra did prefer to be in control.

He couldn't help grinning at the thought of how he'd started his day. Maybe he could find something else he could control for her. After all, she did appear to enjoy giving up control once in a while.

Parking his golf cart next to the others now parked in front of the building, he hoped Mac had given Lacey a ride down in time to get Selma her cream. Part of him was hesitant to find out, but he'd never been one to back away from an unpleasant situation. Striding through the large glass doors, he approached the front desk where Lacey was talking with a guest. She had on a pale green collared shirt and blue jean with her straw cowboy hat. The guests loved her.

Relieved she'd made it in time for breakfast, or maybe a slightly delayed breakfast, he waited patiently, watching out the window as two couples conversed. He didn't even notice anymore that they wore no clothes. Only when there was a particular tattoo or piercing did he take a second look.

"Catastrophe averted." Lacey's triumphant announcement had him turning back toward the front desk.

He stepped up to it and returned her smile. "Thank you."

She shook her head, her blonde braid falling off her shoulder. "Who would steal a gallon of cream? I mean I could see Whisper taking it to give a mountain lion a treat, but since she hasn't been here in a few weeks, I'm stumped."

He'd met Whisper, the animal whisperer, a few times and couldn't say he was completely comfortable around her. That she would give a gallon of cream to a mountain lion didn't surprise him. The last thing they needed to do was encourage the cat that Hunter and Adriana had encountered on the trails. "I doubt anyone here would be friendly with a wild animal like that. Maybe one of the guests decided to cook in their casita and needed a cup. I can see a person coming up at night and borrowing it."

Lacey chuckled. "I hope they don't bring it back at night or Selma will think she's going loco."

He grimaced. "I don't even want to imagine that scenario."

"At the moment, Selma is in her happy place again."

He smirked. "You mean, she's cooking and grumbling?"

Lacey nodded. "Exactly, and I'm happy I was able to help with that."

"Speaking of helping…" He looked around to make sure no one was listening and leaned over the counter. "Kendra and I need your help."

"Of course. I think I've covered everything for the wedding, but if there's something I forgot, you better tell me now."

That Lacey had taken on the role of wedding planner had been a load off Kendra's shoulders and about the only way he could get his fiancée to agree to a date. He had a big bonus scheduled for Lacey in addition to the added weekly pay. "It's nothing you forgot. It's an unexpected occurrence. Mrs. Lowe arrived here last night."

Lacey froze. "What? No, she can't. We have no rooms available."

He used her own word. "Exactly. We had to put her on the couch in Jorge's office."

"No." Lacey shook her head vigorously. "That won't do at all."

"I was hoping you'd say that. Can you work some magic and get her into a guest casita tonight? Preferably on the edge, away from the rest of the guests?" He looked around again to make sure they were alone. "We don't think she'll be very diplomatic if she meets a nudist."

He was halfway through his explanation when Lacey's fingers hit the keyboard. Her blonde brows lowered as she scanned the screen, which didn't bode well. Finally, after a good ten minutes, she finally sat back and sighed. "There's just no way to free up a guest casita."

Not what he was hoping to hear. "Not even a set of friends who could bunk together for a reduced price?"

She shook her head. "Every casita already has at least four in it and two have five. Remember, we actually bought two cots for those."

He did remember. At the time Kendra was thrilled to invest in a couple of cots to make more guests happy. "So that means we don't have any extra beds around I could move into our house?"

"Not unless you pulled one from the staff casitas, but those with two beds are being used. Oh." Lacey's eyes became shrewd. "We might be able to get two staff to bunk together temporarily until Mrs. Lowe leaves."

He swallowed the urge to tell her Mrs. Lowe wouldn't be leaving. They needed to take this one step at a time. "Do we have any possibilities?" Off the top of his head, he couldn't remember who was in what casita or how many beds he or she had. "It would have to be a female staff member."

Lacey rolled her eyes. "Of course." She paused. "Either that or Chris."

Chris was their masseuse. He also happened to be gay, which made the ladies very comfortable around him. But how would Mrs. Lowe feel about living with him. "Better stick to the female staff."

Lacey frowned, but nodded, clearly not happy with what that might mean. Her fingers hit a button and she perused the screen. Suddenly, she glanced at him. "Uh, this is going to take some time and I believe you have a dance class in five minutes. You did pick up Natasha at the garage already, right?"

Well, shit. This had to be the longest morning of his life. "I was just on my way to do that."

Lacey grinned. "I'm just messing with you. She called me about ten minutes ago and I sent Hunter to get her, but you better get over to the Saloon and open it up. You know she doesn't like it when you're late.

His relief was complete. "Have we given you a raise recently?"

She laughed. "Yes, but I'm always happy to take another one. Now go before you're late."

He tipped his hat at her and headed out the lobby doors. He was never late, but for some reason, this morning was getting the better of him. Jumping into the golf cart once again, he glanced over at the opposite side of the ravine. There was no cart in sight, which meant they could well be coming up the main road to the fork right now.

Careful not to speed, he kept one eye on the path and the

other on the crest of the dirt road toward the barn and Old West town. Once he'd passed the fork, he relaxed until the Old West town came into view again and revealed a golf cart parked and two people standing outside the saloon.

The saloon wasn't finished yet. It had a large bar at one end, but other than that it was just a big empty room with a wooden floor, which was great for the line dance lessons he was having his groomsmen take with him. He planned to surprise his new bride at the reception. Hunter stood on the wooden boardwalk in all black as usual with the dance instructor, Natasha Korbas, a thin woman about their age who always carried a large shoulder bag.

Why didn't Hunter unlock the rolling barn door Kendra had insisted on adding in front of the typical saloon doors in order to keep the critters out? Pulling to a stop, he stepped out, an apology on his lips when the sound of barking stopped him. "What's that?"

Hunter, an Army veteran and now Poker Flat security guard, pointed. "That would be dogs."

"As in more than one?" He stepped onto the shaded boardwalk of the newly constructed town.

"Two." Hunter held up two fingers, his mouth quirking up at one corner.

"Sounds like at least a dozen." Still, not sure why his security guard hadn't unlocked the padlock, he inserted his key and pulled down on it before opening the latch. Then he gave the door a shove on its rollers.

As two dogs raced past him and out into the dirt, the smell of shit assailed him. Now he understood Mrs. Lowe's message to Crystal. "Well, fuck."

Hunter brushed by him on his way down the boardwalk steps. "No, that would be shit."

He turned to watch him. "Where are you going?"

"I'm volunteering to catch the dogs. You can have clean up duty."

By rights, he was the boss and should tell Hunter to clean it up, but this was his fault. If he wasn't so confident in Hunter's capabilities to catch the two little mutts, he might be worried, as well as guilty. Luckily, guilt was all he had to feel.

He glanced at Natasha who looked at him, sympathy in her hazel eyes. "I'll just go over and find out what's for breakfast. I'm thinking there won't be a line dance class today, but I'll be back for your lesson with Kendra." She turned her head away as the scent of dog poop wafted outside. "That is, if you still want to practice."

"Yes. By then, the place should be aired out."

Natasha nodded and stepped off the boardwalk, her cowboy boots making a beeline for the main building and away from the mess before him.

Bracing himself, he pushed open the doors and grimaced.

Chapter Four

Wednesday night.

Kendra stopped in front of Crystal's dark casita. Her stable hand had agreed to share Mac's casita until after the wedding so her mom would have a place to stay. When she'd heard the news, she'd felt as if a boulder had lifted from her shoulders. Lacey was worth her weight in gold.

But now, after hearing her mother sing Jorge's praises for two hours at dinner, she wasn't so sure she shouldn't just put her mother up in a hotel away from the resort. Even as the idea blossomed, it shriveled and died. Jorge and her mom were grown adults with their own cars. It wasn't as if she was dealing with teenagers.

Then again, the way her mother had gushed non-stop made it feel like she was with a teenager.

"Well, do I get to see my new digs or are we going to just sit here and enjoy the view of the outside?"

She shrugged. "Don't you like the outside?"

"Don't be a wiseass." Her mother swung her legs out, grabbed the side bar at the front of the cart and pulled herself out. "I need to unpack and settle in. I hope the amazon brought all my bags down."

She quickly followed her mother then froze. The sound of barking dogs came from inside. A shiver raced up her spine as fear swept over her. She took a deep breath. They were inside. She was outside. "Actually, Crystal brought your bags down in the wagon earlier."

Her mother turned to face her. Even in the dim light of the golf cart lights, her mom's irritation was clear. "She better not have broken anything."

Since she couldn't imagine what her mother might have that could be that valuable, she swallowed her retort. "I'm sure Crystal was careful. She likes having nice things, too."

"What are you standing over there for? Are you gonna open the door or not? This is the right house, right?" Her mother stepped back and looked at it and then at the one next door as if she would know.

Forcing herself to move past her instinctual fear, she stepped passed her mother. "I'll let you in, but I'll need you to put the dogs in the bathroom and close the door, so I can explain a few things."

"You're still afraid of dogs? After all these years?"

She ignored her mother's shock. It was easy for her to be surprised. She wasn't the one with the scars to remind her every time she took off her boots. She wasn't the one who'd been in pain, first, because of the coyote's bite, second, from the infection when Fred wouldn't let them go to the hospital, and third, when the numbness wore off after the operation. Forcing herself to put the key in the lock, she turned it, but held the door closed.

"Freckles and Scruffy are sweethearts. They'd never hurt you."

She shook her head. "That's beside the point. But if you don't want to do that, I can just leave."

Her mother's hand on her arm surprised her. "I'll take care of it."

She nodded at her mom's sympathetic gaze, a lump forming in her throat, keeping her from speaking. Instead, she stepped aside and let her mother open the door herself.

Fear sliced up her spine as it looked like the dogs would escape outside, but her mother corralled them and shut the door. A light went on inside as her mother talked to the dogs, cooing over them then coercing them away.

Kendra leaned against the side of the house. Over thirty years later and she still couldn't shake her fear. There was something too unpredictable about them. She'd rather face their local mountain lion.

The door to the casita opened, and she pushed away from the wall. "All set?"

Her mother nodded. "Come in. This is a lot nicer than I expected."

She stopped herself from rolling her eyes and closed the door behind her. It was quiet, no dogs barking, but she didn't want to know how her mother accomplished that feat. Wade had told her what a racket they had made in the morning, which was far more than she wanted to know. "When I had the resort built, I included these staff casitas. As you discovered, we're from far everything out here out of necessity, so I knew some of my staff would want to live on site."

Her mother wandered into the kitchen that was only

sectioned off from the living room by a counter. "It seems small on the outside. I would have thought it was the size of a single-wide. I could definitely live here."

She swallowed a groan. "This is only on loan. We'll figure something out for the long-term."

Her mother opened the refrigerator. "If you don't have enough housing for me, I could always move in with Jorge."

"Mother!"

Her mom closed the fridge and shrugged. "Just trying to help."

It was less her mom's words and more the sparkle in her eye that concerned her. "I think you should be careful about any relationship until the divorce is final. I can tell you from experience that you'll get more assets if you're not seeing someone."

Her mother waved off her concern. "If you mean that thirty-year-old trailer that he refuses to keep up, well he can have it. So what did you need to show me? My dogs are aching from all the activity today. Who knew being outside on a horse would make me tired?"

She cringed at how sore her mom was sure to be tomorrow. "I'm sure you're anxious for a warm soak."

"Oh no. I need to get my beauty sleep. Jorge is taking me into Phoenix tomorrow."

She stopped on her way into the kitchen. "What? He's got two trail rides tomorrow."

"He's just doing the one in the morning. Crystal's leading the other. He's taking half a day off just for me."

He was, was he? Did Wade give the okay? Probably. Anything to help keep her mom from interacting with the guests, but too much time with Jorge wasn't good. He was a nice man and as good as they came, but he flirted with every female he met, and she doubted he felt like her mother did. After being ignored for so long by Fred, her mother was lapping it up like a bear after honey. She'd give Jorge the heads-up.

Quickly, she showed her mother how to set the timer on the coffee machine and pointed out the food she'd had brought in for breakfast. "I hope you'll be able to carve out some mother-daughter time for me." She smiled, genuinely happy to see her mother, even if it was a too early.

"Of course. Jorge is taking me to the botanical gardens. Doesn't that sound romantic? I'm saving shopping for the mother-of-the-bride dress for you."

The botanical gardens? Her mother could care less about flowers and plants. Growing up they had plastic daisies stuck in the ground in front of the trailer. Her mother said they were perfect because they required no care and looked pretty. They barely lasted a Vegas summer, but that didn't stop her from buying more for the following year.

"Then I'll take Friday afternoon off and we can go shopping."

Her mother looked about to argue, but then nodded. "Yes, we should do it sooner rather than later. I don't need anything too expensive. You must have some of those department stores in the city, right? You know, the ones where they get the name brands for less. I usually find good buys there. I don't need nothing from a bridal place. I don't want you spending that kind of money on me. Betty said her gown for her daughter's wedding was over a hundred dollars! That's just plain stupid."

She covered her surprise with a cough. Of course, her mom would expect her to buy her a dress. She may have wiped out Fred's checking account, but there was probably nothing in it to start with. The man spent his pay check on liquor except what her mom could wiggle out for groceries. "Yes, there are a few of those type of stores. I still need to do my final fitting. The store called me last week, but I've been so busy. Would you like to see my dress?"

Her mom sat on the stool at the counter and shook her head. "I still can't believe you've done so well for yourself. Not only all this." She waved her hand at the high ceiling. "But with Wade, too. I never did like what's his face. This cowboy is a real man."

Of course, her mom hadn't liked Eugene. He'd forced her mom to wear a frilly dress to the wedding that he'd bought and then made her take a "nap" during the reception.

He'd been relieved when she insisted that Fred not be invited. After all, he had married her to make his bosses drool over her chest and get him ahead and Fred at the wedding would have ruined that. She'd been young and naïve and happy to help him. He'd always made her feel like he'd married beneath him, which was more than obvious to her. The divorce had been a blessing in disguise. She'd found her backbone as well as herself after that. She smirked. "Yes, Wade is ten times better than what's his face."

Her mother laughed, the sound loud. "I'd say a hundred times better. I'm proud of you, Kennie."

Her eyes felt unusually moist at the use of her nickname. It had been so long since she'd heard it as well as her mother's praise. Uncomfortable with showing that much emotion, she walked around the counter and stood in the living room, behind her mother's back. "So that's a yes on the dress?"

Her mother swiveled on the stool. "Duh. Of course I want to see you in your dress. You didn't get that old looking ivory color I hope. Just because you've been married before doesn't mean you can't wear white, plus ivory looks lousy on you. Not that you need red or anything, but fuchsia would look good on you."

She swallowed a laugh. "No mom, I didn't choose ivory. You'll see it on Friday."

Her mother yawned. "Good. Now I need to get some sleep. I only had four hours last night thanks to sleeping on that couch."

"Was it uncomfortable?" She'd found old Billy on it more than once before he was fired.

Her mother got off the stool, issuing a groan as she rubbed her butt. "Oh, the couch was good, but waking up when Jorge came in was earlier than I wanted." She wiggled her eyebrows. "But he was certainly a better sight to wake up to than your father."

Too quick to agree with her mother, she didn't comment. "Don't let him run you ragged. You may be sore from riding today."

"I'm not that old, Kendra." She waved toward the door. "Now get. I need to let my sweeties out and get some sleep."

She strode toward the door, but turned before opening it. "Why did you get the dogs? I thought Fred was against any animals."

Her mother's face softened. "Those two scallywags were left in a trailer when some riffraff moved out. Betty came over to tell me about them. That was before she moved out. I guess everyone was talking about the dogs barking in this empty trailer. So I had to see what it was all about, and sure enough, the home was empty and locked up tight with those two sweeties inside."

Her mother shook her head. "I swear some people have no more than two peas worth of brains in their heads. Five men and three women standing around talking about it but none of them doin' nothing. It had to be hundred and five degrees that day and those dogs were barking to get out of that oven. It's not like the asshole who lived there left the air conditioning on. So I walked up to the door and tried it."

"You said it was locked."

"Are you telling this story, or am I?"

She nodded, too curious to delay her mother any more.

"Like I said, I tried the door and found out it was locked. So I went around to the side door, because you know there was one, and that blasted thing was locked, too. The dogs heard me and ran to the second door. That's when I got an idea."

She kept her lips pressed together so she wouldn't interrupt.

"Aren't you gonna ask what it was?"

She quickly jumped in. "What was it?"

Her mother slapped both hands onto her hips. "I could bust a window and the dogs could come out that way. No reason for me to go in that hot oven of a trailer."

She widened her eyes, shocked that her mother would take that kind of initiative.

"There was this big old rock at the end of the path to the front door. You know the kind. They're about ten pounds and painted with a saying? This one said welcome which was a freakin' lie." Her mom snorted. "That lowlife never wanted anything to do with anyone. He wouldn't even buy girl scout cookies from Sally's granddaughters."

Her mom took a breath. "Anyways, I picked up that rock and right there in front of all those idiots, I moved to the bay picture window and I threw it. Busted that big old window like old china. I called the dogs and they came to the ledge. I lifted them out one at a time and they've been with me ever since."

Her mother chuckled. "You know, no one ever did ask how the window got broke. A new couple moved in and had it replaced. They seem nice enough. A hell of a lot better than that asshole."

All her life her mother had talked a good game, but she'd never acted. This was a new side of her and Kendra really liked it. "What did Fred say when you brought the dogs home?"

"That lump on a log sat there in his recliner and yelled at me that if I didn't get them out of the house, he'd throw me out. I told him if they left, I'd leave. The son of a bitch was too drunk to do more than grunt."

Wow, sometime in the last three years, her mother had found her backbone. She was more than a little impressed. "Good for you."

Her mother grinned. "Damned right. Now get out of here. I need to go to bed."

"Good night, mom."

Her mother looked surprised. Then waved her out.

She grinned as she closed the door behind her. No one in their family had ever said "goodnight" or "nice to meet you" or "I'm headed to the store, do you need anything." At least her first husband had been good for something. He'd taught her manners, and he's taught her earlier than her mom, that she could stand on her own two feet. Standing with a hot, handsome cowboy was even better.

Climbing into the golf cart, she headed for home. Usually, Wade filled her in at their office, but since she'd taken her mom out for dinner, it was far past time for him to turn in. He should still be awake though since it was only a little past eight.

Walking into the house, she found it dark, except for the upstairs bedroom. She paused in the doorway, enjoying the sight of her very own cowboy, the sheet covering him from the waist down. Her heart hitched at the sight.

She'd always loved broad shoulders and after a year and a half, the sight of his still made her body tingle. He'd officially be hers in a matter of days. She was so thankful he'd pushed the issue of their wedding. She was so engrossed in the business of the resort that she might have put it off far too long. She was damn lucky to have him. "Hey."

He immediately paused the movie he was watching and looked at her. "Hey, how was dinner with your mom?"

She walked in and sat on the edge of the bed next to him, laying her hand on his thigh. "It was fine, if you don't mind hearing about Jorge's amazing eyes and Jorge's scruffy chin and Jorge's patience and Jorge's skill with a horse and Jorge's kind—"

Wade put up his hand. "Stop. I get it. Jorge is a god."

She sighed. "According to my mother, he walks on water. This really concerns me."

"Me too."

"Really?" Having him agree with her was a surprise. "I thought you were going to tell me they are two adults and can figure this out on their own."

He laid his hand on hers. "To be honest, I thought that as well, but I'm worried your mother may mistake Jorge's charm for real interest."

She stared at him. "Yes, exactly. He's the complete opposite of Fred. My mom is so used to being used that I'm afraid she could fall for him and it would break her heart, not to mention that she just left Fred and hasn't even contacted a lawyer yet to start the divorce."

"Do you want me to talk to him?"

Did she? They were grown adults with children of their own. "Maybe you could just explain to him where my mom is at and your concern for her?"

He nodded. "I can do that. Will you talk to your mom?"

"That's a good question. I'm not sure that would be a good idea. I'm afraid if I say something, she'll tell me to butt out or worse, become more determined to start a relationship."

"You know her better than I do."

She smirked. "I did. But she's changed. I don't know if it's me having this place like she says, or if Fred finally did something that she refuses to let go, but she's found her backbone and I think she likes it."

"Good for her. It's one of the things I always admired about her daughter."

She chuckled. "Not always. I remember a time not long ago that you weren't too happy with me standing up for what I thought was the right thing to do for the resort."

His hand moved up her arm then down to her wrist. "True. But I gots me some learnin' and figured it out right quick, Ms. Kendra." He gave her a goofy smile.

"Now you sound like old Billy." She shook her head. "I do miss him, but he's better off at Last Chance. Lacey says he's found a purpose and hasn't had a relapse yet."

Wade lost his smile. "Speaking of that. We need to hire another wagon driver. I spent most of the day shuttling guests down from the garage."

She turned her hand over and clasped his. "You're right. I'll leave a note for Lacey to get in touch with Dale. How did the Manager's Reception go?"

He grinned. "Perfectly. Selma and Adriana had the usual food and drinks ready and Ginger and Buddy decided to play hosts with me, so everyone had a great time. One couple did bemoan the fact that they couldn't extend their stay into next week, but I told them to talk to Lacey to see about a discount on their next stay."

"Good thinking. I'm happy to use the resort for our wedding, even if it does cut into our bottom line a bit. But I don't want our guests to stop coming because of it."

"Oh, don't worry about that. Ginger had to jump in and tell the couple that the reason they couldn't stay extra nights was because you and I are getting married here. By the time she was done, the guests were so happy for us, I'd be surprised if they remember to talk to Lacey."

She smiled. She'd built Poker Flat with Ginger and Buddy in mind. She wasn't surprised that they were being so helpful. They'd always been her surrogate parents.

"What did your mother say about Ginger being your Matron of Honor and Buddy walking you down the aisle?"

At Wade's question, she looked down at their hands. "I didn't tell her yet."

He lifted their hands, forcing her to look at him. "What are you afraid of? I would think telling her earlier rather than later would be better. She's bound to run into them. We can't keep her from the rest of the resort forever."

She sighed. "I know. I think it's just that now that I'm an adult, I feel guilty for having spent so much time with Ginger and Buddy. I could understand if my mom resented them for it. It was just that Fred made being home hell. I'll tell mom tomorrow when she gets back from Phoenix."

He raised his eyebrows. "Phoenix? I didn't think your mom would want to go into the city."

She stiffened. "You didn't know that Jorge was taking half a day off to bring mom to the Botanical Gardens?"

Wade's eyes widened. "No, I didn't." He frowned. "When Jorge asked if I minded if he took half a day, I didn't even think to ask why. He works hard and deserves to have extra time off if he needs it. What if he *does* like your mom?"

"Well, hell." What if? What kind of say did she have in the matter? It wasn't that she didn't wish her mom a better second chance at love, like she'd had. It was more a fear of what Jorge felt. "They only met today. I think we're getting ahead of ourselves."

"You're right. I'll talk to him and get a feel for what he's thinking. He's always respected you, so I'm sure he's not trying to do any harm."

She nodded as she stood. "I better get back. I still have the month-end financials to review. Lacey is asking for new pillows for the casitas."

He didn't let go of her hand. "Come here." He tugged her over.

Willingly, she bent down and gave him the kiss he wanted. When their lips parted, she whispered in his ear. "Thank you for this morning."

He grinned, but let her go as she pulled away. "My pleasure, ma'am."

She was sure if he'd had his hat he would have tilted it. "No, it was definitely my pleasure." She laughed as she sauntered out, purposefully wiggling her butt like Adriana did, though to be fair, she didn't really have the figure her friend did.

"There's more where that came from!"

Wade's yell as she descended the stairs made her smile. She paused. "Careful or I'll be roping myself a cowboy."

The sound of his bare feet hitting the floor gave her all the warning she needed. Running to the door, she ducked outside and started the golf cart. If he caught her, she'd never get to review the financials.

She'd just hit the gas pedal as a naked Wade emerged from the house. Laughing, she waved as she pushed the cart to full speed.

The man had an uncanny knack of knowing just what she needed at just the right time. Slowing down as she crossed through the fork in the path, she finally pulled into the area in front of the main building.

The sound of laughter came from the bar, the guests and Adriana clearly enjoying themselves. As tempting as it was to grab a soda and be sociable, she resisted the urge and headed straight into the now quiet building.

Her cowboy boots sounded loud as she walked down the hall to her office. Actually, it was their office now and soon everything she'd built would be both Wade's and hers. He'd offered to do a pre-nuptial agreement because his assets were substantially less, but everything she owned was tied up in Poker Flat Nudist Resort, while he had cash. As far as she was concerned that was even better.

Now all they had to do was make it one more week and they would finally be legal. For most couples, the final week would usually be fun with family as they gathered and taking care of all the last-minute plans, but nothing ever went according to plan at Poker Flat.

CHAPTER FIVE

Thursday

"I know you want to help, mother, but coming this weekend wouldn't be helpful." Wade strode toward the stable manager's office, his phone to his ear. He wanted to talk to Jorge before he left on his morning trail ride.

"How can an extra pair of hands not be helpful? Your dad could help you with that reproduction coach you were telling us about. You know your father is itching to see it. And I could help Kendra with the seating. That could be overwhelming for her with so much of our family attending."

He paused outside the building. "We're counting on that help, but not until Monday."

"Wade, you obviously know very little about weddings. Three days before isn't enough time to take care of all the details. In fact, I think Jean and Lowell should come. They had a beautiful wedding and would be so helpful."

He leaned against the building. If his mother thought his wedding would be like his sister's high-class affair at the country club, she was going to be disappointed. "I told you, it'll be a simple wedding. People can sit wherever they want and we don't need more than a day to hook the horses to the coach and practice with it."

Jorge stepped out of the office and waved to him on his way to the barn.

"Oh Wade, you're such a man. You just don't understand all the details. It's obvious you need us. We'll head out on Friday after your father finishes with the new patio."

He watched the stable manager head into the barn, probably to help Crystal saddle the horses. The pads Kendra had created for naked horseback riding could be tricky. He really needed to talk to the man. "No, Mom, don't. We don't have any place for you to stay. Besides, dad will be tired after a long day outside. Just—"

"Oh, you're right. Forget that. We'll leave first thing Saturday morning. We should be there by early afternoon. Your sister and Lowell should be able to do that as well. You should see Tierney now. She's getting so big. It's settled then. We'll all see you Saturday."

At his mother's words, he forgot about Jorge. "No, wait. You can't. We'll still have guests here."

"Oh, don't worry about us. We can be quiet. They won't even know we're there. Now I've got to run. I have a fitting for my gown in twenty minutes and it takes thirty to get there. See you soon. Love you."

The call ended, and he stared at his phone. How did that just happen? Was this how weddings always went? He didn't remember his sister's going this way. Then again, all he'd had to do is drink with his future brother-in-law at the stag party then put on a tux and show up for the wedding and eat at the reception.

Kendra was not going to be happy about this. Had his mother completely forgotten Poker Flat was a nudist resort and the closest hotel was a half hour away? Shaking his head, he pushed away from the wall and started for his golf cart. About to get in, he paused as two other carts headed toward him. As the naked bodies of four guests became clear, he tensed. "Shit."

He remained where he was, hoping they would head toward the reproduction Old West Main Street for an early morning massage with Chris, but no such luck. As they headed toward the barn, he sighed and dropped into the golf cart driver seat. He was too late to talk to Jorge.

Turning on the cart, he regrouped. He'd come back after the trail ride. He headed for the main building. Hopefully, Lacey could finagle something for his parents. If not, he'd just tell his mom she could book a room at a hotel.

Yet even at the thought, he knew he couldn't do that. His mom would be hurt. Why was she so anxious to come to a nudist resort? It didn't gel with what he knew about his mom at all.

As he approached the reception desk, Lacey, in her pale pink blouse and matching cowboy hat, smiled. "Just the man I wanted to see."

"Really?" Hopefully, that meant good news.

"Yes. I'm receiving a few wedding gifts in the mail from those who can't make it. Where would you like them? In your office or at your house?"

Not bad as far as news was concerned. "At our house."

"That's what I thought. Now was there something I could help you with?"

He grimaced. "Yes. I just found out my parents and my oldest sister with her family will be arriving Saturday afternoon."

Lacey's grin froze as her brown eyes widened. "Well, sugar, doesn't that just throw a wrench into the cog."

He nodded, keeping in his chuckle at Lacey's version of a curse as she immediately jumped on her computer. "This would be easier if the Ditzmans hadn't returned."

He widened his eyes. "They came back?" He thought they'd be so upset at the resort because of the snake that they'd leave and tell all their nudist friends how dangerous a place it was.

Lacey nodded distractedly as she typed. "Yes. I sent Chris to get them and by time they came back they were so charmed they decided to stay."

He grinned at that. Chris was extremely good at customer service.

Lacey moved her gaze from her computer to him. "So ideally, your family will need two casitas."

"Ideally, but even if you can manage one, we can bring in some cots and they can rough it for a night."

"Right. You do know Kendra wanted me booking the resort right through Sunday."

He did know. "If you can't make it work, Kendra and I can give them our house. We could always bunk down here if we have to."

Lacey frowned and shook her head. "No, I can't let that be the solution. Let me see what I can do."

He gave a quick bow. "I'd be mighty appreciative, ma'am."

She chuckled. "Please, that may work with the guests, but not with me. Now let me get to work on this."

He grinned and headed for the main doors.

"Wade!"

At Lacey's yell, he stopped and looked back.

"Don't forget you have to pick up your tuxedo this afternoon."

"I won't." He continued outside, glancing at his watch. Perfect timing for picking up Natasha for their secret line dance lesson. He couldn't wait to see the look on Kendra's face when he and the guys danced for her. He may have two left feet learning how to waltz, but he'd found his niche with the line dancing.

In no time he was ascending the ravine toward the three-sided garage. He'd reluctantly agreed to Lacey's idea for him and Kendra to learn to waltz for their first dance, and that was only because Kendra looked so interested. He knew that at her first wedding, she had no idea how to dance and her groom had used that as an excuse to cut it short and work the room with his busty bride.

Wade still couldn't believe Kendra's ex-husband had invited clients to their wedding. This one would be totally different. Only close friends, family, and staff would be there. They'd be married under the pavilion and enjoy a relaxed reception in the dining room. Kendra had met his immediate family already. He just hoped she didn't become overwhelmed by having them all together.

He stopped the cart in the shade of the packed garage and waited as the car coming down the dirt road came closer. It had actually been Chris' idea for him to try line dancing. Chris had been to a friend's wedding shortly after Arizona made same sex weddings legal and he'd participated in a similar surprise for one of the two grooms.

Kendra would be shocked based on how badly he waltzed. Wade grinned. She had insisted on them not spending money on gifts for each other, so he was all in on this. For a woman with a nice bank account, she was very careful with money. Mostly likely from the way she grew up and the catastrophe that was her first marriage. Though her mention of a honeymoon had been a relief. She worked too damned hard, driven to make the resort successful.

As the dance instructor squeezed her little car into the covered space, he inched the cart forward. "Good morning."

Natasha gave him a half-hearted smile, a far cry from her usual warm greeting. She was only about thirty herself but had danced professionally for several years and now taught on the side. From what he'd learned, she worked at some kind of call center fulltime.

She walked to the cart with a large quilted shoulder bag where he knew from experience she carried her small speaker. As she sat, she avoided looking at him, focusing instead on settling her bag on her lap. That in itself was unusual.

"Everything all right?"

She nodded, but didn't look at him.

"So that's a no."

At his statement, she snapped her head around. "I'm fine."

Well, shit. Her eyes were red-rimmed from crying. He was never good with tears. He'd never even seen his soon to be wife cry, and for once, he was thankful for her ability to mask her emotions, but Natasha was a dance instructor, not a former poker player.

Starting the cart, he tried to leave it alone, but damn if he didn't hate to see a woman in tears. "Man trouble?"

"What? Oh no. I don't have time for them." She waved her

hand as if his whole sex was far more work than they were worth. She just might have something there.

"Trouble at work?" He had about three seconds before it was obvious he'd hit a bullseye with his second shot.

Natasha nodded her head and sniffed, but didn't say a word. Instead, she brought her fist to her lips and took deep breaths through her nose.

Now he'd done it. He couldn't leave well enough alone. Except it wasn't well at all. "What's up at work?"

He focused on the last switch back before the bridge that straddled the small stream at the bottom of the ravine, but when his dance instructor hadn't spoken, he glanced her way to see tears falling down her cheeks.

Bringing the cart to a stop before the bridge, he faced her head on. "Tell me."

She sniffed. "It's my problem. I'll handle it."

"I have no doubt you will, but everyone needs a helping hand once in a while. I guess you could say that's kind of the Poker Flat philosophy."

Her brow furrowed as she finally looked at him. "I thought this place was about being free from judgement."

He shrugged. "That, too, at least for the guests. But for those of us who live and work here, it's something else."

Natasha cocked her head as if she tried to read his mind. Obviously deciding he was trustworthy, she gave him a short nod like she did when teaching them to line dance, though he didn't get that affirmation very much in the waltz lessons.

She stared him straight in the eye. "I was fired." She let out a big breath as if it was a relief to tell someone.

"Ouch. I don't know how you can be fine after that."

She shrugged, but looked away. "I'll live. I just have to figure things out and find a new job as soon as possible."

An idea started to percolate, but before he got ahead of himself, he needed more information. "If I'm prying, you don't have to answer, but why were you fired? From what I've seen, you're a very hard worker." He grimaced. "And patient, too." He couldn't see the woman yelling at a caller or anything.

She didn't respond immediately. Instead, she clutched the bag on her lap harder. "It's my own fault. I was late one too many times. They had been very understanding, but they said it wasn't fair to the other employees."

Late? She was always right on time for their lessons. Something wasn't adding up. "Why were you late?"

She swallowed hard then looked at him, her eyes misty again. "It's my mom. She's in an Alzheimer's facility. I go over there to have lunch with her. Sometimes when I start to leave, she freaks out and I have to stay to calm her. When that happens, I'm late for my shift." She wiped the tears from her eyes with her finger, careful not to smudge her make-up. "Most of the time she doesn't even know who I am, but when she does, she becomes petrified that I'm leaving her."

His heart constricted at her story. The poor woman. He wanted to help if he could. Poker Flat only hired people who needed a second chance. "If you find another job, how will you keep from being late again?"

She sucked in her bottom lip as she thought about his question. "I guess I'll have to work a night shift. I had hoped to avoid that so I could still teach on the side. My mother's care is expensive."

That wouldn't work for what he was thinking. Still, he'd talk to Kendra about it. "Speaking of teaching, I better get us up to the Saloon."

She gave him that short nod before looking forward again. "Yes. Dancing always clears my head. It will help me figure things out later."

He stepped on the peddle again and the golf cart rolled across the bridge and up the other side of the ravine, his mind churning as fast as the wheels were spinning. Natasha could be their new driver. He'd be happy to show her how to hook up Sage and Daisy to drive the wagon to the garage. Of course, if she did that she'd have to work early morning to evening when either Hunter or Mac went on shift. If she worked at Poker Flat, they could offer their guests line dance lessons, too.

As the ideas flowed, he navigated the resort paths and pulled to a stop at the new Old West Town.

"How does the saloon smell?"

He chuckled at Natasha's sudden question. "Like bleach."

She smiled a real smile for the first time that morning as she stepped from the golf cart. "I'd rather that than the scent we had with your last waltz lesson."

He grimaced, moving toward the rolling door. As he inserted the key into the padlock, he sensed more than heard Hunter stroll toward the boardwalk. Unlatching the lock, he rolled the old barn door to the side and stepped inside, making sure no surprises awaited them.

Once confident no critters or their messes were waiting for them, he held open the batwing door. "It's safe to enter."

Natasha swept by him, depositing her bag on the bar.

Hunter followed. "Hmmm, the smell of clean barracks."

He gave his security guard a wry grin. "I don't know anything about that, but as good as it smells compared to yesterday, I won't mind some of the scent dissipating. I feel like it's taken up residence in my nose permanently."

Hunter nodded as if he was familiar with scrubbing down a room with bleach, but Wade didn't ask.

The sound of boots coming down the boardwalk alerted him to Chris's entrance before he pushed the doors open. "Howdy, pardners."

Natasha gave him an eye roll before plugging in her speaker.

Wade nodded at their masseuse. "New boots?"

Chris tipped a new cowboy hat. "Yes, sir. I figured you all would be wearing them to the wedding, so I wanted to look the part. If we're going to impress the boss, I mean bride, I think we should be as uniform as possible."

He swallowed a flippant remark at the thought behind Chris's actions. "Thank you. I appreciate that as well as you joining in." He looked at Hunter. "You, too. You didn't have to jump on board with this crazy idea."

Hunter shrugged. "Not a big deal."

"Are you kidding? This was a great excuse to look the part." Chris winked. "As soon as my new jeans come in, I know I'll have all the guys checking me out."

Ah, the real reason for the new clothes. "Is this the first time you've worn cowboy boots?"

Chris stuck out his heel and turned his leg right and left. "Yeah. I didn't expect them to be so comfortable."

Wade caught Hunter's eye and raised his brow in question. Should he tell Chris about the boots?

Hunter gave a short shake of his head.

He understood Hunter's reasoning. Chris was obsessed with being healthy and irritated the hell out of both of them at meal times when he criticized what they ate. Better to let him discover how long it would take to break in cowboy boots on his own.

"Are you ready, gentleman?" Natasha's voice put an end to the conversation.

They spent the next forty-five minutes going through the line dance called Boot Scootin' Boogie. He liked the song and the dance. The moves made sense to him, a specific pattern in a regular beat. It was like meat and potatoes as opposed to how he thought of the waltz, Cordon Bleu and legumes, foreign and confusing.

"Good work." Natasha strode toward the bar to turn off her speaker. "You three are almost there."

"Glad that's over." Chris dropped down on the floor and yanked off his new boots. "I think I've got blisters on my blisters."

Hunter shook his head. "A cowboy always breaks in his boots before wearing them all day."

"All day?" Chris stood, his white socks already showing some red dots, proving he'd powered through the lesson despite the blisters. "That wasn't even an hour."

Feeling a little bad for not warning him, Wade gave him a pat on the shoulder. "By the way you danced, I would have never known. Good work."

Chris grinned, his perfect white teeth showing. "Thanks. I'm going to do you proud at the wedding reception, no matter what."

Now he really felt bad for not warning him. "I appreciate that."

Walking past Chris, he stopped at the bar and addressed Natasha. "I'm heading to the office. Would you like a ride?"

"Thank you. I would."

"I'm heading to bed." Hunter touched the brim of his hat. "Night all."

"I'm going to soak my feet before my next client." Chris grimaced before heading down to his massage studio, or as it said on the door, "Sheriff Office."

Wade had a feeling Chris had been itching for an excuse to dress like the rest of them, even if he was the one to insist that he dressed as any professional masseuse. Wade headed the golf cart toward the main building. "How are my brothers and Dale doing?"

Natasha smiled. "They all have your rhythm, but Dale has two left feet. No, let me rephrase that. He seems to have some confusion over what is right and left."

He chuckled. "Yeah, that's been a life long struggle for him. Don't judge him on that alone. He's got a few strengths that make up for it."

"Like loyalty and friendship."

He grinned. "Exactly."

Natasha returned his grin. "He never lets a class go by without singing your praises. I get the feeling he wants me to know you're a good guy even if you do work on a nudist resort."

He shook his head. "People will judge no matter what. Him telling you it's okay to work for the manager of a nudist resort, wouldn't change your mind if you really didn't like the idea, right?"

"No, but I'm not sure it's me he's trying to convince."

Wade forgot to keep the weight of his foot on the pedal and they slowed down. Dale wasn't comfortable with Poker Flat being a nudist resort? It hadn't occurred to him since his friend had been supplying Kendra with employees. Natasha had to be wrong.

"Wade, are we stopping for a reason?"

At her question, he shook his head and pressed the pedal down. "Sorry, I was just thinking about something."

They continued in silence until he stopped the cart.

"Thanks for the ride." Natasha stepped out and threw her big bag over her shoulder.

As she entered the main building, it occurred to him that she didn't mind the nudist resort atmosphere. Every day since they'd started the secret line dance lessons, she'd eaten a late breakfast in the resort's dining room with whatever nudists might have slept late.

Did Dale's concerns arise from his professional business side or a personal side? Shaking his head, he left the cart and strode toward the outside bar, located on the south side of the building, near the pool and next to the large pavilion where he would be married. The bar wasn't open yet, so he'd check on the evidence of a ground squirrel Adriana had told him about. The last thing they needed was a squirrel chewing on an electrical cord and getting fried.

The last bartender Dale had sent had been fine with the nudists, but not so good at bartending. The woman had lied on her resume. The places she'd worked at, which were also resorts, had only acknowledged the dates she'd worked there. After two weeks of training, it was clear she'd never bartended. It had been Lacey who used her connections to discover the woman was actually in housekeeping.

Kendra was more forgiving than he was and had moved the

woman to what she did best. She'd actually been relieved. She was desperate for a job to support her son, but Dale hadn't known they needed another person in housekeeping. So Adriana was back to being their sole bartender and if she needed him to check a desert critter, he was happy to oblige.

Kendra walked down the hall toward the front desk. Lacey would be leaving soon and she needed to find out if she'd been able to make arrangements for Wade's family. His mom's anxiousness to be involved was heartwarming. She must really have no problem with them running a nudist resort.

"Holy cow. Lacey, did you see the bump on that guy's penis?"

At her mother's loud exclamation, she picked up her pace.

Lacey immediately stepped in. "Oh, no, not you Mr. Efford I was just showing her some photos from another resort in this catalog. Have a good evening."

Kendra came to the end of the hall as it opened into the lobby in time to see Mr. Efford opening the door for his wife. Turning, she took the three steps toward her mother as the woman opened her mouth to argue and grabbed her arm. "Mom." She kept her voice low, but made her anger clear.

"What?" Her mother turned startled eyes toward her.

She counted to five as the tall glass lobby doors closed on their guests. "You can't criticize people's bodies here."

"I ain't criticizing. I was just pointing it out to Lacey."

Letting go of her mother's arm, she sighed. "Then you have to do it in a whisper."

"Why? When Betty had that growth on her nose I told her about it and good thing I did because it was cancerous and she had to have it removed. What if that thing on that man's dick is cancerous?"

"I'm sure Mr. Efford can see his own penis."

"Well, he should get it checked out."

At her mother's reasoning, she wanted to bang her head against the wall.

"Mrs. Lowe, I think what Kendra is trying to say is that people who come to a nudist resort come here to be free of being judged. They accept all body types and all scars and marks as natural. In fact, some call themselves naturalists."

"Are you saying that man is proud of his wart?"

Lacey nodded. "Yes. We have even had women here who have beat cancer by having both breasts removed. They are proud to still be alive and their husbands are, too."

Kendra watched as her mother digested that information and steeled herself for what was sure to be a completely illogical response.

"So this is a place where they get to show off then? And every one of these nudies thinks marks and stuff are a good thing?"

Lacey nodded again.

Her mother shrugged. "Well, to each his own, but you won't find me walking about with no clothes. What I got up here," she cupped both her breasts and lifted, "is for me to see and whatever man I think deserving." She dropped her hands and lowered her voice. "And that Jorge may be just the man."

"Oh, that's right." Lacey's smile returned and by her perky attitude, it was clear she was back in receptionist mode. "You went to the botanical gardens today with Jorge. What did you think of the plant life we have here in the desert?"

Her mother waved her hand. "I've lived in the desert all my life. Seen enough of them cactus and mesquite to write a book about them. It ain't the plants I was looking at. Believe me when I tell you, that man's ass is a much better sight." She leaned into the front counter. "I can't tell you how many times I found a reason to step behind him. If he wasn't so much a gentleman, I'd spent the whole day gazing at his behind. But he never walked in front me."

Her mom looked at her. "Your father always walked off without me. I think half the time he forgot he was married to me."

That was an understatement in more ways than one. "I'm glad you enjoyed your time with Jorge. He's always a gentleman with *all* the ladies." Hopefully, her mom would take a hint. "Have you had dinner yet?"

"Oh no, I'm still too full. We stopped on the way back and he brought me to a Mexican place. That's not my favorite food, but since he was paying, I didn't argue. Turned out there were some things they had that I liked. Stuffed myself silly."

"Was there something I can help you with, Mrs. Lowe?" Lacey cocked her head, her single braid falling to the side.

Her mother looked surprised. "Oh, no. I was just going to ask where my daughter was."

"Since you found her, I'll be getting home to my husband. He's a firefighter so he's not home every night, but he is tonight."

"Well, get your hiney out of here then, girl." Her mother waved both hands at Lacey. "Don't want to keep a hot man waiting." She winked. "See, I know he's hot because he's a firefighter." Her mother's laugh filled the tall lobby, echoing off the glass wall.

Lacey wiggled her eyebrows. "You just wait until the wedding. Then you'll see how truly hot he is." She winked before turning and disappearing into the back room.

Kendra listened for the sound of flip flops, figuring her mother's laugh may have caused a couple curious guests to investigate, but all she heard was Lacey gathering her things. She turned back to her mom. "You were looking for me?"

"Yes. I got back and walked Scruffy and Freckles. I wish there was a fence around that casita."

"What did you do at home? Last time I was home, there was no fence."

"I walked them around the park and visited with neighbors, but that's paved. Here it's all desert. I don't want them to get bit by a snake or snatched up by a coyote."

Kendra stiffened.

Surprisingly, her mom patted her arm. "Sorry. I forgot. Anyway, after walking them, I decided it was time to see this place."

Pleased at her mother's interest yet nervous about what she might say to guests, she wished for the hundredth time that her mom had flown in Monday like she was supposed to. "You want a tour? Now?"

"Sure. No time like the present. I've got nothing better to do."

But she did. She had payroll to approve and a package to check on and a dozen other things, but she hadn't spent time with her mom in two years. "Then let's start here." She opened her arm toward the hall. "I'll show you where my office is so you can find me since I practically live there." She lowered her voice. "I'll show you the behind the scenes areas that guests can't see."

Her mother's eyes lit with excitement and she straightened her shoulders. "Of course. I should know more than guests. I'm the owner's mother."

Kendra couldn't take offense at her mother's sense of entitlement. Not when she appeared so proud. She led her down the hall and showed her the staff area behind the front desk, the office she shared now with Wade, and the laundry area.

Her mother's eyes widened at the pile of clean towels and sheets waiting for tomorrow's staff. "That's a lot of bed changes. Glad *I* don't have to do it."

She turned out the light. "I know this is the boring backhouse stuff. Let me show you the rest." She led her mother down the hall, slowing her pace so she didn't pull "a Fred" and leave her mother behind.

Next, she brought her into the dining room, where two guests sat by a window having ice cream sundaes with Selma's homemade churros. Her mother didn't bat an eyelash, her focus set on the doorway to the kitchen.

On one hand, Kendra wanted to tell her mother not to say anything about Jorge, but it would probably go better without mentioning him at all. As she pushed her way into Selma's sacred place, she was struck by the quiet. Instantly, she relaxed. Selma must be on a break.

Quickly, she showed her mother the kitchen and briefly explained the sprayer over the sink and its role in bringing her and Wade together.

From the dining room, she took her mother into the Great Room, the river-rock fireplace the main focal point.

"Would you look at that." Her mom stopped, her mouth

dropping open in awe for a moment. "It's like a Boy Scouts dream come true. Did you build the building around the fireplace?"

She chuckled. "No, but I had to fight for it. My architect thought it was too much, but everyone loves it and even he agreed. Some nights when it's cold, we get a good roaring fire going."

"You'd have to just to keep all these naked people warm. Bet it eats up wood like it's going out of style."

Her mother was so used to pinching pennies, she saw everything as an expense. "It's actually rather efficient. I had to clear out a bunch of debris just before we opened because it hadn't been used yet, but it's worked well ever since."

They strolled past the couches and coffee tables, the side wall of windows showing a number of people enjoying the conversation pool. Kendra distracted her mom by talking about the indoor bar.

"Do you make enough money on the drinks?"

Her mother's question surprised her. "Yes, why?"

She pointed at the outdoor bar. "I see you've got one of them Mexicans working the bar. Never been to a bar with one of them slinging drinks."

Kendra felt her poker demeanor slipping into place to avoid blowing up at her mom. "That's Adriana and she's American, just like Jorge. She's a very good friend of mine. I sell more drinks when she's working than any other time because the guests love her."

Her mother seemed to think about that, then nodded once. "Then that's good. I want to meet her."

Was her mother prejudiced? She'd never heard her say anything like that before, but Fred was an asshole and may have filled her head with stupid ideas. Then again, she seemed smitten with Jorge. "Now remember, when we go out there, you can't say anything about what people's bodies look like. Save it for when we're alone."

"Yeah, I got that message before. Come on, I want to see that pool and fake river you got out there."

Taking a deep breath, she pushed open the tinted glass side door that led to the pool and outdoor bar. Her mother beelined it for the pool. It was a large square with some water features, but the best part was the wide, shallow winding-river piece that came off of it leading up to the outdoor pavilion and ending with a small fountain. A bench was built into the sides and small round tables rose above the water level sporadically along it.

Her mother stood in silence taking it all in. "It's beautiful."

Her mother's words were so quiet, she almost missed them. But then her mom turned toward her, and she'd swear her eyes were misty. "Was this your idea?"

She nodded.

Her mother's face went from awestruck to smug in a second. "That's my girl." She pointed to her temple. "Always thinking." She scanned the entire area then gave a short nod of approval. "Okay, let me meet this Adriana."

"Of course." They walked up to the bar and Adriana, dressed in her usual cut off, ass-revealing shorts and cropped top tied just beneath her breasts, immediately broke off her conversation with a guest and came over. "Adriana, this is my mother."

Her very sexy bartender lifted up the bar top and stepped out. "Mrs. Lowe, it's a pleasure to meet you."

Before either one of them knew what Adriana was about, she'd wrapped her mother in a bear hug, her mother disappearing behind a wall of black long hair. Then her friend stepped back. "I guess I know where Kendra got her sexy rack from."

Her mother burst out laughing, causing the guests at the bar to look over. "You bet. I like to think it was one of the best things I gave her. That and my brains."

"Oh, we are on the same page then. Your daughter is smart and sexy."

Kendra smiled politely, not excited by the focus on her.

"Why are you dressed like a prostitute? Is that why people like you so much?"

She cringed, but Adriana laughed, the sound low and sultry.

Bending low, Adriana responded close to her mother's ear. "You *are* smart. I used to be a very expensive prostitute."

Her mother's eyes widened. "Really?"

Adriana nodded, her dark eyes sparkling with mischief as she straightened.

"Was it fun?"

At her mother's question, Adriana's eyes widened before she laughed. "Yes, it was. I had my choice of hot men."

"What about the old fat ones?"

"Mom!" Kendra scanned the area, hoping no one heard her mother's remark.

"What? I'm curious."

"Mrs. Lowe. Tell—"

"Call me Donna. I'm getting rid of that name as soon as possible."

Adriana looked over her mother's head. "And so are you."

Kendra relaxed. "Yes, I am. I have to say, I'm very happy about that, too."

"Okay, Donna. Tell you what. I have to get back to work, but we'll make time for a girl chat while you're here and I'll tell you everything, including my most recent adventure with heavy cream."

She frowned at Adriana. So that's where the cream went. Wait. She raised her eyebrows. "You're going to tell her everything?" She couldn't help voicing her question, not sure how much her mother should know. Adriana had experienced sex in more ways than all the women at the resort in a year.

"Absolutely. Donna may be your mom, but she's a sexy woman herself. I'd be honored to share my knowledge."

At Adriana's wink over her mom's head, she relaxed. She could trust her friend to be selective, though knowing Adriana, there was bound to be fall out from that particular conversation.

"Yes, get back to work and make my girl some money."

"Whatever you say." Adriana gave her mom a warm smile before sashaying back behind the bar.

At the same time, her gaze caught sight of Ginger and Buddy exiting a desert trail toward the conversation pool. Shit, she hadn't told her mom about their role in the wedding yet. "Would you like to see the Old West main street we built?"

Her mother frowned. "You mean that long set of buildings opposite the barn? I've already seen them."

"Even inside?"

"I thought it was just for show."

She shook her head and linked her arm with her mom's as she led them toward the front of the main building and away from Buddy and Ginger.

"Who's that?" He mother pointed at Chris as he strode toward the main building though it looked like he was limping. Their masseuse wouldn't use the golf carts because he wanted to stay fit, or so he said.

"That's Chris. He works in the Old West town."

"He doesn't look like a cowboy. He looks more like one of those guys on the commercials for those exercise machines. That man has some serious muscles."

That was true. Chris did workout in the weight room, which they'd set up in the bank section next to his massage studio, which was in the "Sheriff Office" store front. When he'd first suggested the weights, she'd had Lacey do the research on nudist resorts having an exercise room and had been surprised that it was common. She'd only bought two pieces of equipment at first, but had such good feedback that they added three more last fall.

The young man approached.

"Chris, I'd like you to meet my mother."

Chris gave her mom a wide smile showing his perfect white teeth. "It's a pleasure and an honor to meet you, Mrs. Lowe." He gave her mother a slight bow.

"Well, aren't you a Mr. Clean with hair."

Chris looked to Kendra in question. He was far too young to know the reference.

"It's an old television commercial. She thinks you're an Adonis."

The man's grin grew. "Thank you. I try to stay in shape."

She gestured toward the Old West Town. "Are you done for the day?"

He sighed. "My last appointment cancelled."

"Appointment?" Her mother tore her gaze from Chris's arms and looked at her. "What appointment?"

"Chris is a masseuse. He gives our guests massages."

"Naked massages?"

Chris nodded. "Yes. It's a pleasure massaging people who aren't nervous about covering themselves."

"I've never had a massage."

Her mom's words brought home exactly how limited a life she'd led. Something Kendra hadn't thought of before. It made her heart hurt that her mom had been confined to that stupid trailer, but she was out now and she deserved to experience everything. Okay, maybe not Adriana's *everything*, but a lot more.

Chris stood with his mouth open. The poor man thought a life without massages wasn't worth living. He finally found his voice. "Then we must rectify that immediately."

"You mean you want to give me a massage?" Her mother's voice rose an octave in her surprise.

He looked to her. "That is, if Kendra doesn't mind."

"I think it's an excellent idea."

Her mom frowned. "Do I have to get naked?"

Chris shook his head. "You do whatever makes you feel comfortable."

"Why not? I'm ready to try all sorts of new things."

Chris held out his arm. "Shall we?"

Without a second thought, her mom grasped his arm and walked away, her voice carrying as she asked Chris question after question.

Kendra watched the two until they'd crossed the fork in the road, her eyes misty with unexpressed emotion.

Two arms encircled her waist from behind, very familiar arms.

"What are you looking at?" Wade's voice was low, his lips close to her ear.

"My mom, but through new eyes."

He turned her around to face him. "Whoa, are you going to cry? I've already had one teary-eyed female on my hands today. I'm not sure I could handle another."

She blinked the moisture away. "No, I'm not going to cry. You know me better than that. But now you have to tell me who was crying and what you did to help, because I know you and my perfect cowboy would feel obligated to help. However, I'll tell you this, if you held her in your arms like this, you're sleeping on the love seat tonight."

He chuckled as he shook his head. "Not to worry. No touching was needed. Actually, you're the one who could be of help."

"Me? I would think a female nudist would much prefer a handsome cowboy's help."

"It wasn't a nudist. It was Natasha."

"Oh, was that why she was so lenient with you during our waltz practice today?"

He pulled his head back. "Why wouldn't you think it was because I'm improving with the waltz?"

She gave him a small smile. "Because you have two left feet. But it's okay, I love you anyway."

He grinned before lowering his head to kiss her. It didn't take long before it turned hot and her belly tightened with need.

"Get a room you two!"

At the sound of Buddy's voice, she broke the kiss and looked around Wade's shoulder. "Us? You're the ones walking around naked."

Wade dropped one arm and turned to face them, his other arm still around her waist. "And don't get used to it. Starting Saturday, my parents arrive."

Buddy grumbled, "I thought we had until Monday."

Ginger, a middle-aged woman with bright red hair who had been her surrogate mother, beamed. "I, for one, can't wait to meet them. I just know the in-laws will be wonderful."

Kendra coughed. "Um, speaking of family, my mom arrived yesterday."

Ginger threw both her arms up in the air. "That's wonderful. Where is she? Why haven't we seen her?"

Wade squeezed her waist in silent encouragement.

"She's been out with Jorge. I wanted to tell her about you two, but haven't had a chance yet."

Buddy frowned. "Why do you need to tell her about us? I'm assuming if she's here, she's a nudist."

She shook her head. "No, she's not, and thank you very much for putting that image in my head."

Buddy smirked. "You're welcome."

"But sweetie, you don't mind us being nudists. Does your mother not approve?"

The fact was, she wasn't sure about this new mother of hers. "I don't think she has a problem with it since I showed her around today. It's just that she's changed. As in, I'm not sure I know much about her anymore."

Ginger patted her hand. "I'm sure it's just because you haven't seen her in what? Two years?"

"Oh, it's a lot more than that. She's left Fred, has two dogs, a crush on Jorge, and wants to live here." She hadn't meant to blurt it all out, but Ginger and Buddy had provided her the family life she never had and were the inspiration for Poker Flat.

"Wow." Buddy's quiet comment said it all.

It didn't clarify anything, but just having two other people who understood what a big change that was made her feel saner. "Yes, exactly."

"Well, you just let us know when you'd like us to make an appearance. We don't want to cause problems between you and your mom." Ginger smiled kindly.

"Thank you, but I don't think it's a problem. I just don't know what she's going to say next."

Buddy chuckled. "At least that much hasn't changed."

She silently agreed.

"We're going in for dinner. We had a long hike on the new desert trail. It's lovely and the views are amazing. What great exercise."

"Yeah, if you like sweating."

Ginger latched onto her husband's arm. "You had no problem with that last night."

Buddy, to his credit, turned red. "Come on. Are we going to eat or not? I'm famished."

As he led his wife toward the entrance of the main building, Kendra tried to imagine her and Wade at that age. Somehow, she couldn't see him blushing. Then again, she couldn't see both of them walking around nude. They may do it for the weekly manager reception, but they agreed they preferred their clothes on in public. In private was a whole other matter.

Wade slipped his arm from her waist and grasped her hand. "I have to agree with Buddy. I'm hungry and Selma made three-cheese enchiladas with refried beans for dinner."

She stared at him. He had charmed Selma from the first day he'd arrived at the resort. "Now how do you know what Selma made for dinner?"

He gave her the crooked grin of his that she so loved. "I asked."

Oh, there was much more to it than that, but that was between her madam-turned-cook and her husband-to-be. "I'm hungry, too. Can you bring it into our office? Showing mom around put me behind. I still have those two ad packages to review."

Wade winked. "Your wish is my command."

At the subtle reminder of the morning her mom arrived, tingles invaded her body. "Hmmm, I can think of a few times where it was the opposite."

"It's almost all I think of."

She laughed as he opened the door for her. Once inside, it was obvious what Selma had made for dinner as the scent of enchiladas filled the lobby.

Wade let go of her hand and headed for the dining room. She couldn't help but watch him, her fascination with his broad shoulders alive and well. How the hell did she get so lucky?

Chapter Six

Friday

Kendra glanced at the time on her computer. It was only one in the morning and she'd accomplished everything she'd hoped to do, but she couldn't go to bed yet. She was wide awake and Wade was sleeping. Their opposite sleep and work habits made having sex a fun challenge.

She grinned at the memory of the first time she'd "ridden" him in her office after a strip poker game. That was before the resort had opened, but she still managed a few rides now and again, like earlier in the evening after their intimate dinner.

Despite the time that had taken, she was still caught up, probably because the resort was closed next week. Part of her was happy for the break, but the business side of her balked. Still, it *was* her wedding. If there was ever a reason to close the resort it was that.

It wasn't as if she didn't have more money from her poker winnings and subsequent investments. She could support the resort if she had to, but she wanted it to sustain itself and eventually make money. In essence, it was her retirement.

She hadn't really thought of it that way in a long time, but having her mom wanting to live with her put a new spin on things. Her mom basically had no skills, no income, and no home. To make matters worse, she would soon be spending a lot of money on a divorce, unless Fred decided it was easier to give up a housecleaner than give up his money.

Of course, that meant she'd have to support her mom until she could collect social security. How long would that be? Ten years? Yes, ten years if she started early.

She couldn't imagine her mom, and her two dogs, living at Poker Flat that long. Maybe she could find her mom an apartment in the closest town?

Even at the idea, her stomach clenched. Her mom would be insulted to be pushed out of Poker Flat. "Shit." Snatching up her cowboy hat, she plopped it on her head and strode out of her office, locking the door behind her and heading for the bar. She needed a beer.

Walking through the empty Great Room, her cowboy boots made far too much noise for her to hear if any guests were still outside with Adriana. Pushing open the side door, she stopped and listened. The sound of glasses being washed floated toward her, but no voices and no guests in sight.

Walking over to the bar, she sat on one of the stools.

"Hey, what are you doing out of your office?" Adriana looked at her bracelet watch. "You're not allowed out until the vampires take over."

She chuckled. "I know. I'm surprised, too. Can I get a beer?"

Adriana turned around and pulled her favorite from the cooler. After opening it, her friend opened a case to grab a cold mug.

"No, don't dirty another glass. I'll drink it from the bottle."

"Whatever you want." Setting the beer on the bar, Adriana scooped some ice into a glass and used the soda nozzle to pour herself a ginger ale.

Kendra lifted her bottle. "You're not going to join me?"

"No. I've gotten in the habit of avoiding beer or any alcohol since I learned about Hunter's wife. He's pretty touchy about it."

Hunter's tragic story included deployment, a permanent injury and a drunk driver. When she'd hired him, she never thought he and Adriana would fall in love, but they did. "Do you think he'll have a problem with the wedding reception? It's open bar and I'm sure even those who don't usually drink are bound to imbibe too much, especially since everyone will be staying here."

Adriana took a sip and put her glass on the bar. "I actually talked to him about it. We decided that if he couldn't keep his cool, we'd leave."

She nodded. "That's a good plan. I don't want him to be uncomfortable. He's an excellent security guard and I'd rather not lose him."

"Excellent?" Adriana smirked. "He's the best."

"I don't know." She winked. "Mackenzie is damn good."

Adriana nodded. "Sure, for a woman. She's beyond fit. I think she's the only woman who might be able to outlast me in bed." She held up her hand. "If I wasn't with Hunter."

Shit, that said a lot about how far Hunter and Adriana had

come. Adriana loved sex and while she'd enjoyed men, she wasn't averse to women, too. She must be serious about her relationship.

How had she missed that? Probably because she was buried in her office all the time. She needed to get out more.

"Will you ever tell me Mac's story?" Adriana wiggled her brow. "You know I won't tell."

"Why don't you ask her? You must see her when she—" Her phone's ring interrupted her. At this time of night, it couldn't be good. Pulling it from her back pocket, she tensed. "Hunter."

As Adriana's focus sharpened, Kendra answered. "What is it?"

"It's Chris. You need to come to the garage."

"On my way."

Hunter hung up before she did.

"What did he say? Is he okay?" Adriana's concern was telling.

"I'm assuming he's fine, but not sure about Chris. Hunter didn't exactly elaborate."

Adriana blew out air from between her full lips. "He never does. Just call if you need help."

She stood as she took a bracing swig of beer then ran to her golf cart parked in front of the main building. Jumping in, she pushed the pedal to the floor and drove toward the fork in the path.

If Chris had been out drinking with friends and came back drunk, Hunter might be barely holding his temper in check. She needed to get there before he lost it. Then again, Chris could be hurt. No, it sounded like he wanted her to pass judgement as if Chris had done something he shouldn't.

She was getting better at understanding Hunter's tone of voice. The man's lack of conversation meant understanding his tones. To give him credit, since he and Adriana had started living together, he'd loosened up a bit, even smiling on occasion.

The golf cart rolled across the bridge before she directed it up the other side of the ravine. She focused on the switchbacks, the incline twice as steep as the side where she built the resort.

When she reached the top, she drove around the barricade that kept people from driving over the cliff and turned toward the three-walled garage. In the dim lights of the golf cart, she could see Hunter and Chris standing next to Chris's sedan, his back-passenger door open.

Now what was that all about?

Stopping her cart, she stepped out and looked at first Chris then Hunter. "What's wrong?"

He jerked his head toward Chris.

She turned toward her masseuse. "Spill."

Chris didn't even hesitate. "I was at a bar in east Phoenix. My blind date had picked it as a neutral place to meet as it's very popular."

She could sense Hunter already growing bored. He must have heard the whole story already.

"I noticed these guys watching us. They had that look. You know, the one that says you should be ground into the Earth and then lit on fire?"

She had to admit she hadn't been a recipient of one of those stares. "What happened?"

Chris looked toward his vehicle. "He saved me."

That Chris' words were breathless as if he was still in awe wasn't lost on her. "Who saved you from what?"

He turned back to her. "After Jay and I exchanged numbers

and made plans for another date, he left. I had to wait longer for my tab. As I exited, I could feel these guys watching me, so I moved a bit faster than usual." Chris looked at the vehicle again. "I literally jogged down the steps before I heard the door open behind me. I didn't look back, making a beeline for my car, but they were fast."

She could feel the fear coming off her employee even as he spoke. Her protective instincts rose hard. "Did they hurt you?"

He shook his head. "They didn't get near me. There were five of them."

She sucked in her breath. Chris was strong, but no one could fight off five men.

"They surrounded me, taunting me. Like I haven't heard it all before. You'd think rednecks could come up with new material about gay men. Seriously."

She held back her grin at Chris' change in demeanor. He was better educated than she was and had little tolerance for idiots.

"Anyway, I figured I'd have to make a run for it. I picked out what I thought would be the two slowest men to run between, when I heard a truck door slam. Three of my adversaries looked in that direction and that's when I went for it."

Kendra tensed. Though Chris stood before her unscathed, she couldn't help worrying about him.

"I almost made it, too, but one of them grabbed my shirt. I swung at him and caught him in the jaw before another grabbed me. That's when Kane showed up." Chris gestured toward his car. "He didn't say a word. Just started dropping them one by one, until they finally figured out their only chance was to gang up on him. They released me and ran for my car."

Cain? As in Cain and Abel? Wasn't Cain the one who killed his brother? She shook off the thought and focused on Chris. Since Chris was a relatively new hire, she was surprised by his willingness to let a man, even one named Cain, take the blows meant for him without helping. "You left him?"

Her employee frowned. "This isn't the first time I've been in a tight spot. This is still the old west after all, but no, I didn't leave him. I crouched behind a car and hit the app on my phone. It's the sound of a police siren that sounds far away but gets louder as if it's getting closer. I have it set for two miles." Chris grinned. "You should have seen those idiots scatter. Kane was still standing until one of them gunned his car right for him. I pulled him out of the way, but he still got clipped."

Kendra stared at Chris, trying to process the scene in her mind. What he'd described was a hit and run on top of assault and battery. They needed to press charges. They needed to—

"He wants to bring him home."

At Hunter's words, she faced him. "Home?"

Her security guard nodded toward the car. "He's a mess."

Chris shook his head. "Kane wouldn't let me take him to a hospital, so I convinced him to let me take him back to my place." He pointed behind her. "But Hunter said I had to get your okay. I tried to tell him who I bring back to my place is no one's business but my own."

"You mean you have this Cain in your car?" At least a dozen ramifications of Chris bringing his hero back to Poker Flat ran through her mind and she shifted her weight to her right leg.

"Yes." Chris squared his broad shoulders. "After he stepped in to help me, it was the least I could do."

That was true. However, they knew nothing about the man. He could be a convicted felon. Then again, she already had one of those working for her. And to be fair, the man *had* stepped in to help Chris without even knowing who he was. That indicated a good moral compass. It was more the fact that the man had been *dropping* the others, as Chris said, that concerned her. Someone that good with their fists could be dangerous. "And his name is Cain as in Cain and Abel?"

Chris took a breath as if trying to be patient with a child. "Not that it matters, but it's spelled K-a-n-e. As in the movie Citizen Kane, though my defender is nothing like that character. I think Kane's a cowboy." The last word was said on a sigh, Chris' gaze becoming unfocused as he stared off into space.

"Chris, are you interested in this man?"

"Oh, to be so lucky. But I'm destined to admire from afar."

"Huh? What's that supposed to mean?"

Chris' gaze snapped back to her. "He's not gay."

"He told you that?"

"No. I just know." His shoulders fell. "Such a waste."

She bit the inside of her lip to keep from grinning. She'd never heard a gay man use that particular phrase. She had to wonder what Kane would think of Chris' admiration. The last thing Chris needed was to be accused of improper behavior again. Maybe Kane should be driven to his own home.

She looked back at Hunter to find him not there. He'd moved to Chris' car and was bent over with his head in the open door. Just the sight of him reminded her that she had him, Wade, and even Mac to help if Kane ended up being a problem. Chris was technically correct. She didn't have a right to tell him who he had over to his casita. If Kane did have a criminal past and caused trouble, she also knew a detective that would be happy to haul him away. She started toward the car, intending to lay down some ground rules, when Hunter backed away and a man stuck his arm out, using the door to help him stand.

As he braced himself, Kane exited the vehicle.

Well fuck. The man had to be over six-foot and he was built like a football player. As Kane turned and looked in her direction, she doubted he could even see her. His eyes were both swollen from the beating he'd taken on Chris' behalf. Kane also had a cut on his cheek, his nose was bleeding, and his arms in the white tank he wore, were full of cuts as if someone went after him with a knife. His dirt covered blue jeans were ripped on his left thigh, and he held what looked like a denim shirt in his hand.

There was no decision to make. "Hunter, help him into my golf cart. We need to get this man into a bed."

Hunter didn't say a word. He just placed Kane's arm around his shoulders and guided him toward her cart. Once Hunter had him settled, she turned to Chris. "You did the right thing, though a hospital would have been better."

"No hospital." At the sound of Kane's quiet voice, they all looked at him, but he didn't say anything else.

Chris held both hands out to his sides. "Told you."

Fine, no hospital…for now. "Let's get you both back to your casita." She left Chris and strode toward Hunter who stood waiting next to the cart. "Thanks for calling me."

Hunter nodded then stepped back.

It was a clear signal he'd done his job and the rest was up to her.

She appreciated that. When she'd first hired Hunter, she was afraid he'd balk at taking direction from a woman, but she'd learned his superiors in the Army had been both male and female. Of course, she also had Wade who was the resort manager, but it was good to know her employees still acknowledged her as the owner of Poker Flat and the final authority.

Looking back at Chris to be sure he was settled in the back, she turned on the golf cart and took her passengers down the ravine at a much slower pace than she'd come up. Without the moon, the only light was from the small headlights on the golf cart which illuminated a very short distance. Even so, the man next to her didn't tense. She just hoped he didn't fall out before they made it to Chris's casita.

Once there, he was Chris' responsibility. Even so, she planned to check with Lacey in the morning to see if they had any medical professionals staying on the resort. She'd like a second opinion on whether he should go to the hospital, and she would damn well find out why he didn't want to go.

<center>~~~~~</center>

"One two three. One two three. Wade, there's no four in the waltz."

At Natasha's reprimand, he stopped. "Sorry. It's hard to concentrate with a beautiful woman in my arms." He gave Kendra a crooked grin.

"Oh, no, don't try to charm your way out of this." Kendra's own lip quirked up in the corner even as she shook her head. "Unless, of course, you want to be the one to tell Lacey we aren't going to waltz for our first dance as bride and groom."

He raised his brow. "How did we get talked into doing this anyway?"

She shrugged. "Oh, I'm sure it was something about how beautiful we'd look and how everyone would sigh and realize we were meant to be. Or some such nonsense."

He shook his head. "If Lacey wasn't such a miracle worker, I'd quit right now."

"That miracle worker found your family a casita to stay in tonight, so I suggest you try again."

"I agree." Natasha strode over. "If you're having such a problem counting with your fiancée in your arms, then try it with me."

Shit, that wasn't what he wanted. He needed to keep his big mouth shut. He glanced at Kendra as he took Natasha into his arms. His soon-to-be-wife was smiling smugly. He'd get no help from that quarter.

"Now on the one beat. Ready, and…"

He kept the count in his head. He didn't want to embarrass Kendra at the reception. She had enough qualms about his family. Though he'd been teasing about not being able to concentrate, it amazed him how much easier it was to focus with Natasha. He was a pathetic lump of mush when it came to Kendra.

"Okay, now move me into the turn." Natasha nudged him by pressing his hand.

He took the hint and stepped around, moving her in a circle. As they danced by Kendra, he grinned at her.

When she rolled her eyes, he chuckled losing the count and stepping on his teacher's toes.

"Ugh. Okay enough."

He immediately released Natasha and stepped back. "I'm sorry."

Natasha waved it off. "You're not the first and you won't be the last. Let's stop for today." She looked at her watch. "I'd like to leave a little early anyway. I have an interview."

"Already?" He clamped his mouth shut. Insulting his dance teacher was probably not smart.

"Yes, though I'm not excited about the job. It's factory work, which is fine, but it's night shift. If I get it, I'll have to give up teaching dance."

He looked at Kendra, who was frowning. They had talked about Natasha, but the dance teacher hadn't given Lacey her resume yet. Maybe she didn't want to work on a nudist resort. "You can always interview here."

At Kendra's startled look, he shrugged.

Natasha put her speaker into her large over-the-shoulder bag. "If I don't get this position, I definitely will."

Ignoring Kendra, he decided to dig a little. "Have you ever ridden a horse or driven a wagon with horses."

Natasha's eyes grew round. "Oh no, I'm afraid of horses. I can't even get within ten feet of them without breaking out in hives." As if she recalled where she was, she forced a smile. "No offense, but if a job here entails that, I better keep looking."

Kendra brushed past him, elbowing him in the ribs before approaching Natasha. "If you have a resume on you, leave it with Lacey at the front desk. We do have a couple positions open at the moment. After *I* see your resume, we can talk."

He was in for it now. Kendra was pissed, and he had an idea why.

"Thank you. I'm going to run over and grab some lunch before leaving. I don't want to arrive at the interview with my stomach growling. Besides, I saw Selma had fish tacos on the menu today. I love those. Been making those since I was tall enough to reach the stove."

"You eat tacos?" Though his question sounded stupid when it came out of his mouth, he just didn't see the thin, put together and graceful Natasha munching down on messy tacos.

She laughed, the first time he remembered her doing that since they'd met her. "I may have traveled with my career, but I grew up in Arizona. Tacos were a staple." She threw her bag over her shoulder. "I'll see you tomorrow."

As she walked out of the saloon, he turned to face Kendra. She was looking at him, no expression on her face whatsoever, her weight on her right hip. "If you're angry, show me. Don't use that poker face with me."

She threw her arms up. "Fine. What the hell were you doing? You practically tripped over yourself trying to offer her a job. We have a process here. If she can't get her resume to me first, then I'm not talking to her."

He crossed his arms over his chest. "I wasn't tripping over myself. I just know how distraught she was yesterday. We already know she's punctual, patient, and doesn't mind being around nudists. I just wanted to remind her that we have openings. Though I had hoped she could drive guests and their luggage down in the wagon."

Kendra looked away. "I know. I could tell what you were thinking, but for all we know, she has excellent accounting skills or customer service rapport and could take over for Lacey. I can't know that until I see her resume."

He studied his fiancée. Something wasn't right. The whole conversation, even Kendra's quick anger wasn't normal. "What's wrong, and I mean what's really wrong."

When she didn't look at him, he knew he'd nailed it. Dropping his arms, he strode toward her and stopped in front of her. "Look at me."

After a heavy sigh, she finally did. "What?"

"Tell me what's bothering you."

She looked away again and shrugged.

"Come on, tell me. I'm about to be your husband. We can't have secrets. Or is it the wedding that has you on edge?"

"No. Yes. I mean, the wedding stress is one thing but…"

He remained silent, but captured her waist in his hands. Gently, he squeezed.

Finally, she looked at him. "It irked the hell out of me that you could waltz fine with Natasha but can't get past ten steps with me. What's that about?"

He swallowed hard to keep from laughing. "I told you the truth. When I'm holding you in my arms, I get distracted. You have to understand, I have a unique view of you from here." He purposefully looked down her buttoned shirt.

She snapped her head down and gasped. "That's what distracts you?"

He chuckled. "Among other things, like feeling your body against mine, holding your hand, breathing in your almond-rose scent." He could tell the minute her anger left as her body relaxed.

She ran her hand up the front of his shirt and unbuttoned the top button. When her fingers slid beneath the material, his cock responded. Kendra didn't have the long nails or extra soft hands of the other women he'd been with. Everything about her was strong and practical and it always made him hot.

"Is this distracting?"

He pulled her shirt from her jeans and ran his hand up her smooth back. "Very."

Her hand found his nipple beneath his shirt and as she pinched it between two fingers, his balls tightened. He lowered his mouth to hers and swept his tongue inside.

Mine. The word flew through his head. It had been happening a lot lately. Deep in his gut he was worried Kendra would create a reason to call off the wedding. While she seemed to want to get married, the actual wedding made her nervous. The only way he could think to ease them both was to show her exactly how much he loved her.

As she sucked on his tongue, his thought process ceased and his body took over. He crushed her to him, tasting her, feeling her, pressing his erection into her belly. He forced her to back up until her ass came into contact with the empty bar.

She moaned at the contact and his need to taste more than her mouth overpowered him. Leaving her mouth, he started a trail of kisses to her cleavage. Scooping his hands beneath her ass, he lifted her onto the bar, bringing her large breasts to the perfect height for his attentions.

He licked at the side of one breast as his fingers worked on opening her shirt. He'd just pushed aside one cup and lifted the nipple above the material when footsteps on the boardwalk outside reminded him where he was.

Kendra stiffened, but unable to help himself, he grasped her nipple with his teeth and sucked it into his mouth.

"Wade." Kendra's voice was more of an inward breath.

The steps came closer.

He sucked hard, pulling his mouth away slowly until he caught the hard nub between his teeth.

The steps were loud now and he finally let go, to face the person who had interrupted his play. His cock was rock hard and an obvious bulge beneath his jeans and he didn't care. Since the saloon was the last doorway on the boardwalk, that meant the person was looking for them, and he planned to tell him or her to go away.

He'd barely taken one step toward the doorway when they were thrown wide and Abril, their new waitress and mother of three stormed in.

"I quit."

That was the last thing he'd expected, so it took him a moment to refocus. "What?"

"You heard me. I quit. Your cook is loco in la cabeza. She's back there throwing pots and screaming louder than some hyena. I need a job but not that bad. *Adios*." She threw up her hands and stormed out of the saloon.

He turned to look at Kendra. Their thought was the same. "Selma."

"Fuck." Kendra jumped off the bar, buttoning her shirt as she headed for the door.

He held one side open for her and joined her. "You want me to talk to her?"

Kendra's strides were long as they headed for the main building. "Yes. We need to find out what set her off. She hasn't thrown a pot since the first day I let her into the kitchen and Sheriff Harper butted his nose in there and started asking questions about sanitation." Kendra's mouth quirked up. "He never set foot in there again."

"Maybe it's that simple."

"I hope so. Where'd Abril go?" Kendra looked for their waitress, obviously hoping to talk her into staying.

He scanned the area, but didn't see her anywhere. They weren't that far behind her for her to have disappeared so— "There." He pointed toward the other side of the ravine at a golf cart starting up the switchbacks.

"Oh, that's not good." Kendra's worry was evident in her voice.

When a pair of guests ran from the building, he and Kendra started to run.

Lacey came out after the guests. When she saw them, she shook her head. "I think she's lost it."

He nodded as he opened the door.

Just inside was Natasha. "I tried to talk to her, but she's not lucid. Her emotions have completely taken over."

"Thanks." They ran into the dining room and stopped.

"Mom?" Kendra looked at her mother who was crouched down behind a table that had been pushed over on its side, broken dishes littered the floor around her.

"Thank God, you've come! That woman is insane! She needs to be locked up!"

At Donna's raised voice over the din in the kitchen, Kendra nodded at him and he strode for the open doorway.

"Come on, mom! Let's get you out of here."

He walked into the kitchen and assessed the situation in an instant. Selma waved the iron skillet in her hand while screaming obscenities, reminding him of a bull he'd fallen off in a rodeo long ago, who had turned on him ready to do serious damage. Then a rodeo clown had run interference. This time, it looked like he was the clown and poor Jorge the target.

Despite his better judgement, he stepped between the two. "Selma. What's going on?"

At the sight of him, she took a breath. "Ese hombre puta. Él es una mierda de mierda. That man-whore. He's a cock-sucking piece of shit. He needs to be stripped down and flayed with hot irons and that still wouldn't be enough of what he deserves. Voy a golpearlo sin sentido y le cortaré la lengua del diablo!" To punctuate her statement, she reached over to the stainless-steel cutting table and grabbed a large knife.

Shit. He didn't know that much Spanish, but he knew enough to figure out Selma was pissed at Jorge for something and planned to do him bodily harm. Not taking his eyes off their cook, he turned his head. "Jorge. I suggest you leave. Now.'"

"Si, I've been trying. Gracias."

As Jorge moved toward the doorway, Selma's focus switched. She turned to follow, but Wade blocked her way. "No. You need to calm down."

Her eyes widened in surprise. She gestured toward Jorge. "Él está lamiendo su coño when he knows my heart is set on him. Then he flaunts her in my face in *my* kitchen. I'm going to cut off his dick and stuff it down his throat!"

At the sound of Jorge's boots walking across the dining room floor, Wade relaxed a little. It was time for the charm that always worked well with her. "Now Selma. If Jorge is such scum, why do you waste your breath on him? You're a beautiful woman. You could have any man you want."

The woman spit on the floor, which wasn't a good sign. She was proud of her clean kitchen and right now it looked like a battleground between the dented pots and the broken glassware. Kendra was going to be furious.

"He was mine until *she* showed up. What she doing here? He spend all his time with her. I make her pay. No puta is going to take my man."

"My mother is not a whore."

The cold sound of Kendra's voice behind him had him stepping aside. She looked as furious as he'd guessed, and he wouldn't stand between her and her employee. Selma had been a madam in Nevada who lost her place and Kendra had offered her a job at Poker Flat, but friendship only extended so far and how to handle the situation was her call. He'd just stay nearby to make sure she wasn't hurt.

Selma had stopped ranting at Kendra's announcement. From the look of the older woman's face, she was struggling with her options. *Come on Selma. Back down. Apologize.*

She did neither. She turned her back on them and waved her hand. "Get out of my kitchen."

"This is *my* kitchen. I allow *you* to work in it."

Wade braced as Selma turned around slowly, not oblivious to the pan and knife still in the older woman's hands. He wanted to caution Kendra, but she was well aware of Selma's temper.

"What?"

"I said. This is *my* kitchen and I allow you to work in it. But you've obviously forgotten that."

Selma's brows lowered and her resemblance to that bull

from his past had him shifting his weight, ready to protect Kendra.

Selma turned to the left and threw the pan and knife toward the wall where Jorge had been, the knife sticking solid as the pan clattered to the floor. "Fine. You can have your fucking kitchen." Without another word, she ripped off her apron and stormed past Kendra and out into the dining room.

They stood frozen, listening to the loud footsteps of their cook stomping out.

Letting Kendra handle that without stepping in was one of the hardest things he'd done. His whole body felt like a rattler ready to strike, but whose head had just been cut off.

Kendra let out her breath. "That was stupid." She looked at him. "Are you sure you want to marry such a stupid woman?"

He covered the three steps that separated them, his heart, still pounding at the danger she could have been in, twisted at her comment. "You're not stupid. You did the right thing." He wanted her to be confident in her decision. She'd made so many about the resort up until now and she's done well.

"Now what are we going to do?"

He gave her a crooked grin. "What we always do. We figure it out."

Her shoulders slumped and she gave him a grimace. "Lacey won't be happy."

"I'm sure with four business days still left, Lacey can work her magic and get someone to cater the wedding. Our bigger concern will be dinner tonight."

Her brow puckered. "How far away is the closest pizza place?"

He wrapped her stiff form in his arms. She was tense and

would need time, but just touching her helped him relax and think. "You had to go and say pizza. Now I have a craving."

She shook her head against his shoulder and he was positive she rolled her eyes even if he couldn't see it. That alone was a good sign.

"Excuse me. I just wanted to make sure you two were okay."

Kendra broke away and faced Natasha. "Yes. We survived." She looked around the room. "Though I'm not sure our kitchen did."

Natasha's eyes widened as she scanned the room. "It will take some doing to get this cleaned up in time for dinner."

"Since we no longer have a cook, I don't think that's going to be the issue." Kendra pulled out a stool at the end of the prep table and sat. "Unless you know someone who can cook chicken enchiladas in the next…" she looked at her watch, "three hours, I'm thinking it's going to be carry-out pizza."

Natasha opened her mouth then closed it.

Wade's gut prompted him. "Did you have an idea? We're wide open to them at the moment."

Natasha looked at her own watch then at the kitchen again. "If someone could help me clean this mess up, I could make the enchiladas, if you'd like."

"What about your interview?" Kendra recovered faster than he did.

Natasha shrugged. "I think you need the help more than I need the interview. I'll call and see if I can reschedule. That is, if you'd like me to make the dinner and if you could pay me."

Kendra looked at him.

He raised his brow. They shouldn't look a gift horse in the mouth.

She turned back and gave Natasha a genuine smile. "We can do that. Thank you. I will send Jorge in to help clean up since it appears he was part of the problem. Wade, if you can man the stables, we could have Crystal come over and help, too. Then you can break it to her that she's back on waitressing duty."

He chuckled. "Break it to her? I think she secretly prefers it. And without Selma to contend with, we may not get her back into the barn."

Kendra rose from the stool. "This just brings home how many more people I need to hire. I'm going to my office. I need to call Dale and crunch some numbers."

He opened one side of the batwing doors and followed his fiancée out into the dining room. Now that he had a chance to look, it was a significant mess. He didn't envy Crystal and Jorge. "I'll find Lacey and see if she was able to smooth this over with the guests."

"Thank you."

As they exited the dining room, they found both Lacey and Donna waiting for them. That made finding Lacey a whole lot easier.

"Mom? I thought you were going back to your casita to rest."

"Rest? There's no time for that. I just changed. I wanted to have easy clothes to take off for trying on a gown. You said we had to leave by three, right?"

"Right." Kendra looked at her watch again. "I didn't realize it was so late already. Let me grab my keys."

By her tone of voice, it was obvious to him, and from the

worried look on Lacey's face, that Kendra had completely forgotten her final fitting appointment. That begged the question. Would she remember their wedding?

CHAPTER SEVEN

Friday continued.

Kendra stood still as the assistant fixed the short veil on top of her head. At the brush of it against her bare shoulders, she frowned. "Where's the bolero jacket?"

"Oh, we had to make some adjustments on it. I'll bring it out to you. I'm sure your mother is anxious to see you."

"She's not the only one." Kendra grumbled under her breath. There was no mirror in the dressing area. She'd have to go out in the semi-private room where other women were being fitted in order to see what she looked like.

She'd ordered the jacket specially made for a reason. Otherwise her large bustline would be the focus of attention at this wedding, too. At least this time, she could pick out her own dress.

Stepping down from the small platform the shop assistant had her stand on, she almost tripped. She couldn't remember the last time she'd worn heels. Being a professional poker player certainly hadn't required it, nor did running Poker Flat. It had to be Cole and Lacey's wedding, but she'd had Wade's arm to help her.

"Be careful. You must hold your dress up when taking stairs. Will there be steps into the church?" The assistant's frown of concern seemed a bit over the top.

"No. We're getting married outside, but the steps up into the stage coach are very high." She grinned at the astonished look on the woman's face before sashaying down the hall toward what she considered the public display room. She really wanted that jacket.

"You don't have champagne? I thought all these fancy bridal shops have champagne." Her mother's voice carried down the hall, making her cringe.

"I'm sorry ma'am. We don't serve it here because we don't want any accidental spills on the brides' gowns. If you like, we have some coffee in the staff room. I can bring you back there."

She turned the corner just in time to see her mother wave the man off. "Never mind. We'll just have to go out and have a drink when we're done here."

The man nodded politely then looked up as he caught sight of her. A large grin spread across his face. She put her finger to her lips since she approached the little platform from behind her mother.

The man gave a quick wink and turned away.

Her dress was strapless with dainty appliques covering the bust and waist area, tapering down to a point on her butt. Other appliques were set sporadically along the skirt of the dress. It fit very tight at the top to keep her breasts in place and followed her figure to about her knees where it flared out then stopped at the floor.

As she passed the couch where her mother sat, she took as deep a breath as she could, bracing herself for what she'd look like in the mirror. Lifting the dress, she climbed the two steps to the platform before the three-sided mirror.

She stared at the woman in the reflection, her own nervous blue eyes looking back at her a moment before she dared to study the dress on her body. She looked like a sophisticated woman.

It was so opposite of who she was that she shifted her weight to her right hip. What would Wade think? What did she think? As she continued to stare, the silence in the room finally registered. She moved her gaze past herself in the reflection to find everyone looking at her. The man who had offered her mother coffee was the only one smiling. Was he laughing at her?

"God, Kennie. You're beautiful." Her mother's words were just above a whisper, which was so unlike her.

Kendra shifted her gaze to her mom, who had risen and was looking at her with tears in her eyes. For the first time since she was a little girl, she gazed at her mom in gratitude, feeling her support no matter what others might think. "Thanks, mom."

As if her words had broken a spell, others in room added their compliments. At first, she thought they were just being nice, but a few of the young brides actually looked jealous. Jealous? She was in her earlier thirties, had a huge bust, wide cheekbones, a wide mouth, and no hips.

She revised that thought as her gaze fell on her jutted-out hip. She looked around for the assistant and found her standing behind the couch. "Is the jacket ready?"

"Jacket?" Her mother's loud voice caused a few irritated looks.

She kept her voice lower, hoping her mother would take the hint. "Yes. I had them make a bolero. It's nice."

Her mother strode forward and stepped between her and the mirror. "What do you need a jacket for?"

"To cover this up." She waved her hand toward her bust. "I don't want to be on display. That's too much like what Eugene did."

Her mother's brow furrowed. "That idiot had the taste of a monkey drunk on cheap gin. This gown isn't even close to that one. That one had a neckline so low we could see your belly button, for Christ's sake!"

This time everyone turned.

She swallowed hard, forcing herself not to shush her mother. She'd learned as a teenager, that only made things worse. Instead, she lowered her voice even more. "I know, but this makes my bust look like I'm a porn star or something."

"A porn star?" Her mother's reaction was too loud to ignore and a few of the people started grumbling.

The man who had offered her mother coffee walked over. "Is something wrong with the dress, ladies?"

Her mother pointed at her. "No, the dress is great, but there's something wrong with her. She thinks she looks like a porn star because of her God given bustline and wants to wear a jacket to cover it up."

"I see."

Kendra doubted very much that the man could see anything, but to his credit, he looked interested.

"Please, turn around full circle."

She raised her eyebrows at him. "Why?"

"I want to see the dress from every angle so I can give you both an impartial, and may I say, expert opinion."

Her mother looked as doubtful as she felt. "Expert? Who are you that you're such an expert?"

"I am the owner of this establishment. I chose every gown in here."

Her mother recovered quickly. "Well, you did a good job on this one. Though I can't say the same for that frilly thing that girl is wearing." Her mother pointed to a young woman who had on a pink bridesmaid's dress which had so many ruffles she looked like a stick of cotton candy.

The young woman across the room grimaced. "I wish you'd been here when the bride picked this out."

Her mother gave the woman a sympathetic frown. "You poor thing."

"Eh-hem." The owner brought their attention back to him. "As for that, I have to order what is requested to keep the *brides* happy. And speaking of happy brides, would you please turn around, miss, so I can give you my honest opinion?"

Rather than argue the point, she began to turn. The man probably did know something about wedding gowns if he owned the shop. And she'd thought him just a salesperson.

Lacey had seemed to know a bit about dresses, too. Kendra didn't even remember which dress Lacey had convinced her was the best for her bridesmaids. Did that make her an uncaring bride?

When she finally faced them again the man was nodding. "Yes, you have the exact shape I was thinking of when I ordered this gown. It's reminiscent of the 1930's sophisticated nighttime galas. You're stunning in it as is. To wear a bolero over it would make it look off balance and dare I say, odd."

Her mother smiled smugly. "See. I told you. You don't want to look odd, do you?"

She studied herself in the mirror again. Wade said he loved her body even more than she did. She would never argue that point. His constant adoration of her and all her slightly deformed parts, be it her leg or her bust, had made her feel more comfortable… around him.

As a teenager she'd hidden her breasts until she'd met Eugene who told her they'd make them successful. Her entire, extensive wardrobe had been low cut neck lines to show off her assets, as he called them. They had certainly helped him sign clients and add "assets" to his own portfolio until he decided he needed a woman from wealth like himself.

Wade wasn't using her. He was sincere in wanting her to be comfortable with her body. Like he said, she only had one and he loved it just as it was. Simply thinking about him had her tension easing.

He would be proud of her if she wore the dress without a jacket. So everyone would see exactly how big she was in some places and small in others. They were all people she knew and if they were coming to her wedding that meant they must like her a little. Besides, her wedding was for her and Wade.

"I'll take it without the bolero."

"Excellent." The owner bowed and stepped away.

"That's my girl. I just know your cowboy is going to love unzipping that back zipper to unwrap you like a lollipop he can't wait to lick."

A woman on the other side of the room, gasped, but the girl in the cotton candy dress grinned. "You roped a cowboy? Good for you." Giving the thumbs up, she turned and headed for one of the dressing rooms.

Kendra smiled at her mom. "Okay. I'm done, now it's your turn."

Her mother's eyes widened. "Not here. You said there was a department store nearby."

She lifted her dress and walked down the stairs. "That's true. But I want only the best for my mom." She nodded toward the assistant. "Please show her any dress she likes."

As the assistant led her mother off, she caught the eye of the owner who gave her an approving nod. Her cynical self told her he just wanted the sale, but her strung tight emotional self decided he was proud of her for making her mom feel special. Giving him a quick nod, she headed for the dressing room. Since she sent off the assistant with her mom, she hoped she could reach the back zipper to take the dress off. If not, they may be in the shop for a long time.

~~~~~

Saturday

"Wade, come over here."

Lacey waved to him as he crossed the Great Room. The day was going far better than he'd anticipated. Natasha had volunteered to continue working as their cook until Dale could find them someone as long as she could take time off during the day to have lunch with her mother. Selma hadn't come near the main building
~~~~~

all day, and the band had called Lacey to confirm the time for Thursday.

He stepped up to the counter. "What can I help you with?"

Lacey, looking very country in her peach checked shirt, white jeans, and white straw cowboy hat, smiled triumphantly. "Look what I found." She set her laptop on the counter so he could see.

"A white harness?"

"Yes, for the stage coach. We could deck it out with white flowers and white ribbons."

He swallowed his chuckle. "It's very nice, but I don't think it's going to go well with Sage and Daisy." The two draft horses were matching blonde Belgians, anything but dainty.

"Why not?" Lacey crinkled her brow. "Do you think the white would clash with their ivory hair?"

Clash? "No, I meant because they're so large. When was the last time you were at the barn?"

She shrugged. "I don't know. Last month? Jenna's horse, Cyclone, is a Clydesdale and I think he'd look great in this."

If he remembered correctly, Jenna was the vet for Last Chance ranch where Lacey lived and where he'd purchased more than one horse. "Then if you think the harness would look good, and it can get here in time, I'm fine with it."

Instead of nodding at his approval of the expense, Lacey frowned. "Do you think Kendra would be okay with it?"

He gave her a genuine smile. Based on how affectionate Kendra had been yesterday evening when she'd come back from her fitting, he'd say she was on board with anything. "Yes, I think she'd love it."

Lacey beamed. "Excellent. I'll order it and have it shipped

overnight. If this stage coach thing works out, we could put together a whole wedding package and advertise it to our clientele."

"That's a good idea…if it all works out."

Lacey patted his hand. "Oh, don't worry. We've got this."

"We?"

She spread her arms out. "All of us. Everyone who works here will make sure this wedding goes off without a hitch. Do you need Jorge's help to maneuver the stage coach out of the building?"

And there went his happy mood. He glanced at the clock behind the counter. His parents and older sister would be arriving anytime. "Not today. My family will be here soon, and my dad wants to do that."

Lacey smiled. "I can't wait to meet them. I have to say I'm impressed that they wanted to help with wedding preparations so much, they are arriving while we're still open."

"Yeah, I'm not sure what my mother is thinking. My niece is three years-old."

Lacey waved away his comment. "Oh, that's fine. From the research I've done, nudists are used to naked children around. It's a natural thing."

Not natural for his family though. "I don't think Jean is going to let my niece run around naked. Which casita did you manage to get them?"

"The one closest to the pavilion, so your parents wouldn't have far to go to attend the wedding."

And they would pass the main building, pool, bar, and four casitas filled with naked people before finding theirs. He just couldn't see his mother being comfortable around naked people. She was known to criticize actresses on television for revealing too much at awards shows. His gut felt like a knot in a rope that had been swollen with rainwater.

"Is something wrong? You don't look happy. Were you hoping for a different casita?"

At Lacey's crestfallen look, he forced a half smile. "No. You did great just to open up a casita."

She shrugged. "I just gave a couple guests a discount and they were happy to share. Oh, and I had a cot delivered. I didn't know your niece was only three."

"That's fine. What's not fine is them coming today."

Lacey's eyes widened. "Why?"

"They aren't nudists. I told my mom we'd have guests, but she just said she'd be quiet. No idea what that has to do with anything. When she gets an idea in her head, there's no swaying her."

"Oh, my. Is she as, um, obvious as Donna."

He grinned. "No, my mother is very polite, but my grandmother has a lot in common with my future mother-in-law. Luckily, she won't be in until after Sunday."

Lacey pulled her laptop around and tapped a few keys. "Tuesday. She'll be here for the bridal shower. I can't wait to see the two of them together. I have a feeling there will be a lot of laughter."

"And embarrassing comments that I'll be happy to miss."

Lacey laughed. "I'll be sure to take notes."

"Great." He let his shoulders slump in defeat before straightening again. "I'm on my way to check on Chris' guest. Let me know when my family arrives at the garage."

"Oh, you don't have to check on Kane. He's all set." She pulled her laptop back down and placed it on her desk behind the counter.

"You found a medical person among our guests?"

"Oh, I did better than that." She grinned smugly. "We have a radiologist and a surgeon here. I went with the surgeon, and he was happy to take a look. He believes Chris' guest has broken ribs, a broken finger, and a lot of bruises. The surgeon splinted his finger, prescribed ice for his ribs and ibuprofen for the pain. He said Kane could confirm the broken rib diagnosis with an x-ray, but based on his pain and restricted movement, the surgeon was pretty confident. However, he told Kane if he started wheezing or had trouble breathing to get to an emergency room, but agreed Kane doesn't need to go to the hospital for any additional treatment at the moment."

He raised his brow. "What about the broken ribs. I had a couple of those during my short rodeo season. If I remember correctly, they taped me up."

Lacey shook her head. "Not anymore. The surgeon said to use the ice and not to move in any way that causes pain. I know Cole's cousin, Logan, had his arm in a sling just to keep him from moving the wrong way. Not sure if that would help Kane, but I'll mention it to Chris."

This was one of those times when Lacey's efficiency actually got in the way. He wanted an excuse to meet the man who had defended Chris without even meeting him. Either he was the hero that Chris made him out to be at line dancing, or he was someone who was always looking for a fight, one of Kendra's concerns. "Great work as usual, Lacey. I think I'll head over there, anyway, to see how—"

His phone rang. A quick glance at the caller told him it was his mother. "Are you here?"

"Hello to you, too, Wade. Yes, at least I think we're here. There's a barricade at the end of the road. Are we in the right place?"

He'd given her directions three times. Detailed directions. "Yes. Just park in the garage you just drove past."

"He said to park in that metal structure." His mother was obviously speaking to his dad. "Okay, then what?"

"I'll be up to get you. Just wait there. It will take me a couple minutes."

"Okay. I don't see anything but desert here. How are you going to get here in a couple minutes?"

He was already walking out of the lobby. He'd parked the wagon at the fork, so he wouldn't have far to go. "It's an optical illusion. Trust me."

"Oh, I see because your guests don't want to be disturbed by the outside world. I understand. We'll wait."

He jumped up onto the bench seat of the buckboard wagon with the modified shocks for their guests' comfort. "See you in a few." Not waiting for his mother to respond, he ended the call and picked up the reins. Flicking them, he started Sage and Daisy down the ravine.

The two draft horses knew the route by heart having brought many a guest down to the resort. The golf carts were only used after dark. However, most guests arrived in the daylight and could appreciate the surprise of Poker Flat.

A sense of pride rose inside. He couldn't wait for his parents to see what Kendra had built. From where they were parked, the resort was completely hidden by the ravine, and where she had placed the barrier made it hard to see the large opening unless a person knew it was there.

When they married, she insisted that the resort become theirs instead of hers. Her willingness to share her dream with him had been humbling. He hoped his dream would be something she'd like to share as well, but he'd have to wait until after their marriage to give her his wedding gift.

Was she proud of him? Sometimes he wondered. She'd been afraid to trust him because she saw him as perfect for the longest time. Though he'd proved himself to be anything but, he could tell she was hesitant about fitting into his life like he fit into hers.

She'd surrounded herself with people who needed a second chance. He hoped she saw this second wedding for her as *her* second chance.

As the horses appeared over the ridge of the ravine, he heard his sister. "Look!"

He grinned once the wagon brought him into view of his family standing in the shade of the garage. They stood with their mouths open, except for his niece who was picking up a rock from the desert floor.

His dad recovered first, a wide smile transforming his weathered face. "Well doesn't that just knock the flies off a cow's ears?"

He laughed, his heart full at finally being able to share the resort with his family. His smile faltered as he remembered the customers wandering about. He had thought to show off Poker Flat to his family when it was empty.

He pulled Daisy and Sage to a stop a few feet away. No help for it now. They were here. Jumping down off the driver seat, he embraced his mother who had recovered from her surprise of seeing him appear out of nowhere. She wore a flowered sundress with half-sleeves that showed off her thin figure. Her pale blonde hair camouflaged the many grays, but she still smelled of lilacs just as she always did. He loved that she never seemed to change.

She stepped back. "Look at that tan you have. Are you wearing sunscreen?"

"Yes, mom." His no sleeve button-down shirts were Kendra's favorites, so he'd worn one for her today, forgetting that his mom might not approve.

She studied his arms then met his gaze. "Just be careful."

"Karen, give a man some room to greet his son." His father, who was only an inch shorter than him but broader gave him a bear hug. When he stepped back his eyes glistened with excitement, proving that his wavy hair may be almost all white already, but his spirit was still young. "You have me more than a little curious now, son."

He shrugged, but couldn't stop smiling. "I told you the resort was built on the side of a ravine."

His father chuckled, "So you did."

A tug on his jean leg pulled his attention. Looking down he found his niece, Tierney, holding on with one hand and lifting a rock with her other. "Here. Here."

Crouching down to be closer to eye-level with her, he held out his hand, palm side up. "What did you find, Tee?"

"A ruby." She smiled triumphantly as she put the brown rock in his hand.

"Is this for me?"

She nodded before turning her head to look at her mom.

Before he could ruffle her short dark curls, she'd let go and run off only to be captured by her dad, who lifted her in the air causing an ear-piercing squeal of happiness.

"It's good to see you, Wade."

He rose from his crouch and gave his older sister a hug.

"I'm happy to see you, too, Jean, though I wasn't planning on it until Monday."

As his brother-in-law, Lowell, came over to shake his hand, he explained the accommodations. "Since we still have resort guests, I had to put you all in one casita. But this one has two bedrooms, so I hope you'll be comfortable."

His mother took his arm. "Oh, we'll be fine." She walked him toward the wagon. "Now I simply can't wait to see Kendra to find out what I can do to help."

As his mother talked, his father and Lowell pulled the suitcases out of the trunks of the two cars they'd travelled in.

He led his mom around to the back then disengaged his arm so he could take down the steps that folded up under the bed of the buckboard. Along each side was a built-in bench with a cushion where guests sat. At the end, there was no seating as that was where the luggage was set, though there wasn't much since their guests didn't bring clothes.

"How quaint." He resisted the urge to laugh. His mother was always polite, no matter what. He took her hand and helped her ascend to the back of the wagon. After piling everyone in and adding the luggage, he locked the back board in place and strode toward the front bench where his father was already waiting.

"I'm sensing a theme." His dad patted the seat beside him. "Very smart."

He flicked the reins and turned Daisy and Sage around to head back to the resort. "Oh, you haven't seen anything yet."

"I'm ready to be impressed." His dad sat back, resting both elbow on the short back of the bench seat.

Maneuvering around the barrier on a well-worn wheel track, Wade kept the horses to a slow walk. When the wagon came close enough to the ravine edge, his father sat forward.

The resort came into view.

"Wow."

At his father's soft-spoken word, he felt the wagon shift a bit as his family turned to look. When the horses reached the edge, he halted them. "Whoa."

"That's impressive." His dad's words sent pride filling his heart. He hadn't designed it, but he'd helped make the resort the success it was…or rather the success it almost was.

From their spot, they could see the whole layout of the resort perched on a shelf on the opposite side of the ravine. The guest casitas dotted the hillside, some almost down to the little stream.

"Wade, this is beautiful. No wonder you wanted to be married here. It's breathtaking." His mom patted his back. "What an oasis. I can see it's a tranquil and spiritual place."

That wasn't exactly what Kendra had been going for, but he'd take it. "To the left over there is the stables, stable manager's office, and coach garage. Across from that is the Old West Mainstreet. Behind that is the staff casitas. The two-story structure is Kendra's home. The right is the main building with Great Room, dining room, offices and indoor bar. As you can see, to the right of that is the outdoor bar, main pool and conversation pool which flows to the pavilion. That's where the wedding will take place. The casitas you see across from the pool are the guest casitas. Lacey has the one closest to the pavilion reserved for you."

He looked back at his sister. "Tomorrow, you, Lowell and Tierney can move into the one next door."

"Wade, this is really impressive." His sister's awe meant a lot. Jean and Lowell traveled quite a bit and only stayed at the best places.

"What are we waiting for?" His father grinned at him. "Let's get these horses movin.'"

At his father's comment, he clicked his tongue and Daisy and Sage started down the slope. His family continued to comment on everything they saw from the stream to the bridge to the signs that told guests exactly where everything was.

He brought the horses to a halt in front of the main building. His father was watching two nudists bring their drinks from the bar to two lounge chairs on the side of the main pool. His eyes were wide with surprise.

That didn't make sense. He and Kendra had told them all about the resort being for nudists. Maybe he was surprised by something else. As his father broke into a wide grin, he relaxed.

Jumping down, he walked to the back of the wagon and took off the back board. Taking out the luggage, he set it on the ground before helping his sister out. He was just assisting his mother down the steps when a golf cart pulled up. The guests exited the vehicle and strode inside the main building.

His sister, who held Tierney in her arms, quickly turned so the girl couldn't see.

His mother's grip in his hand tightened. "Wade. Those people were naked." Her voice was so low, he almost didn't hear her.

"Yes. They're supposed to be." He lowered his brow as his father walked around to the back of the wagon. "This is a nudist resort. I told you that."

His mom's face paled. "Oh, my God."

His dad rested his hands on her shoulders, his mouth quirking with humor. "Actually, I don't think a higher being is really what this place is about."

His mother gave his dad a scathing look.

"I don't understand."

His father had laughter in his voice. "Your mother thought you said Buddhist resort. She'd convinced us all that you and Kendra ran a retreat for Buddhists."

He widened his eyes at his mother. "Is there a large Buddhist population in Arizona?"

She continued to scowl. "I don't know."

A sudden thought, froze him in place. "You couldn't believe that we would run a nudist resort." The cloud of pride he'd been riding all the way down the ravine evaporated as if the Arizona sun had targeted his chest.

His mother's face cleared as she grabbed his arm. "No, honey. That wasn't it at all. I had just never heard of a nudist resort, so I thought I must have misheard. When you and Kendra described it, it just made sense to me that it might be a spiritual escape. They have them in Sedona, so why not here?"

He studied his mother's eyes. She was always polite, even with her own children. Did she mean it, or was she hiding her disappointment?

Another golf cart arrived and Mr. and Mrs. Richards, annual visitors stepped out. Mrs. Richards walked directly to him, and his sister quickly spun around to face them all since Tierney was looking over her shoulder.

"Wade, it looks like you have new guests." The short, slight pudgy, seventy-six-year-old lady had a heart of gold and had been instrumental in helping them start a good reputation.

He forced a smile. "Yes, but not for the resort. This is my family. They're here for Kendra's and my wedding."

"Oh, how wonderful! Adriana told me about it. I just know it will be beautiful. How can it not with such two wonderful people? You must be so proud" She looked directly at his mother, so he made the introduction.

"Mrs. Richards, this is my mother and father."

"Oh, please, call me Lucinda and this is Leonard. I was just thrilled to be one of Poker Flat's first guests. This place is so special and the improvements in just a year are simply amazing. I can't tell you how rare it is to find such a lovely place to vacation. Believe me, not all clothing optional spots are so beautiful, or so well run." She looked back at him and he smiled politely.

"We're very proud of them, of course." His mother gave a polite smile. "We can't wait to see our casita."

Mrs. Richards nodded. "You will love it. We were just going in for some ice cream. At our age, watching our weight takes a backseat to our enjoyment of sweets." She patted her tummy. "I'll let you get settled in. I'm sure we'll get to talk later."

"Thank you. That would be nice."

Mrs. Richards took her husband's hand and shuffled off to the entrance of the main building.

No sooner had the doors closed than his father chuckled. "Well dear. That's what you get for insisting on coming early."

His mom moved out from his father's hands and faced him. "I'm glad we came. Now we can really appreciate all that Wade does here."

Jean stepped forward. "I'd like to put Tierney down for her nap. Can we go to our lodging now?"

His dad shook his head. "Not me. I'm ready to see this reproduction stage coach."

"That can wait." His mother looked back at him. "I'd like to see Kendra and find out where she is with all her planning."

Wade looked at each of them and silently nodded. Things just got significantly more complicated.

CHAPTER EIGHT

Saturday continued.

Kendra strode toward the barn. Selma hadn't been seen since her freak-out, but her car was still in the garage. That concerned her. It was time to get to the bottom of the issue and from the few words of Spanish she understood, Jorge was the bottom.

She stepped into the shaded coolness and inhaled the scent of hay and horses. The open areas on each side of the barn were now for grooming on one side and tack and feed on the other. If a monsoon was imminent, they brought the wagon into the grooming bay. Beyond that were six stalls on each side, and ten of them were used on a daily basis, she and Wade agreeing to hold off on more horses until the demand required it. She hadn't realized how much horses cost to house and feed.

Whistling in one of the stalls caught her attention. The first few stalls were empty, the big Belgians on duty with the wagon and a few out in the corral. As she walked by Sundancer, the horse nickered. She couldn't resist giving him a pat. "Miss me, huh?" It had been so long since she and Wade had ridden out to their secret cove along the stream and made love. Their office was the setting for most of their sex. She missed being outdoors alone with him.

"Someone here?"

At Jorge's question, she continued down past the stalls until she found him cleaning out Elsa's, one of the horses that was out in the corral. The Arabian was smaller than Sundancer and scarred badly from a wildfire, but she was docile and got extra attention from the guests. Again, the wonder at how accepting nudists were of physical imperfections filled her. Why couldn't she be as confident? "It's just me."

"Oh, *hola Jefe*." He tipped his white hat with the back of his gloved hand. "What can I do for you?" Jorge stood straight and smiled as he leaned on the shovel he'd been using. He was a thin, shorter man who was probably a few years younger than her mom, but he had no white hair yet. He was also very honorable as attested to by his slightly crooked nose which he got defending her honor.

"We need to talk."

He lost his smile and leaned the shovel against the wall. As he exited the stall, he opened his arm toward the exit of the barn. "I have two lawn chairs outside. I wouldn't mind getting out of the smell for a few minutes."

She turned toward the barn opening, her boots sounding muffled on the wood floor. Once outside, she noticed the lawn chairs and took a seat.

He sat once she did. "You want to know about your mama."

Surprised by the question, she hid her reaction. "That's a good start."

He looked away to respond. "I like your mama. I never wonder what she's thinking."

She stifled a chuckle at that.

"It's refreshing." He looked back at her. "You know?"

She nodded, not wanting to change his opinion. She found it anything, but refreshing.

"But she's still married and your papa didn't treat her well, right?"

She shook her head. That was an understatement.

"I think your mama just needs some attention, so I give it to her. That's all."

This wasn't the subject she'd come to talk to him about, but now that they were, she felt oddly protective. "But what if she sees this attention as something serious? Long term?"

Jorge's deep brown eyes grew round. "Long term? No, no long term. I was just being nice. Does she think I want something long term?" As the man's tone rose an octave, she was convinced he didn't realize how fragile her mother's heart was.

"I'm not sure, but I think she does. I also think Selma thinks so as well."

Jorge crossed himself and looked at the sky before responding. "That woman is loco. She makes no sense."

"Why do you say that?"

"Because I try to take her to dinner. I bring her flowers. I even fix her window, and she doesn't want anything to do with me. Then I see your mama eating lunch by herself and I join her. Next thing I know, Selma's screaming like la Llorona running out of the kitchen and hurling dishes at us."

Jorge rose out of his chair and faced her directly. "That

woman I don't know. She's not the warm, big hearted woman I think I know. She's someone else. Maybe a bad spirit take her over."

"And maybe it was love." As a professional poker player, she'd learned to watch body language and she'd noticed Selma almost went out of her way to appear extra gruff whenever Jorge was around as if she didn't want him to know she liked him. Kendra had also noticed Selma listening avidly when guests spoke about him.

Jorge stared at her as if she'd turned into a spirit horse right before his eyes. "Now I'm thinking you a bit loco."

She shrugged. "If I'm wrong, I'll have to fire her. I can't have an unstable cook…that is if she hasn't quit. Hard to tell with her."

Her stable manager stiffened at that. "She'll probably come 'round."

Kendra rose. "I don't know. I'll try to talk to her. Give her a chance, but I'm not putting up with that kind of behavior. Everyone deserves a second chance and since this is her first offense, I'll wait and see. But I won't tolerate another."

Jorge lifted his hat and wiped his brow before settling it back on his head. "You're a good Jefe. Selma knows that."

"I hope so. In the meantime, I suggest you stay away from my mother, for her sake, your sake and Selma's." She didn't wait to see if he agreed. Instead, she strode away to where her golf cart was parked. Stepping into it, she turned it on before glancing toward Jorge. He remained where she'd left him, hopefully thinking about a few things.

One uncomfortable conversation down and one to go. Driving past the Old West town, she headed for her mother's casita. She hadn't seen her all day and she needed to tell her about Buddy and Ginger.

When she arrived, she knocked and waited. There was no answer and no sound inside. Hesitant to intrude, especially if the dogs were inside, she knocked again, but all was silent. Wouldn't the dogs bark?

But what if her mom had fallen and was unconscious. The thought had never occurred to her before when her mom was living two states away with Fred, but the idea took hold and wouldn't let go. With no choice, she took out her master key and unlocked the door. "Mom? Mom!"

She took a quick walk through the one-story house before she was satisfied. Locking the door behind her she was at a loss as to where her mother might be with the dogs. It was time to get her mother a phone.

Jumping into the cart, she drove back to the main building. After checking with Lacey, Crystal, and Adriana, she started to get worried. If she had to, she'd wake up Hunter and get him on it. Striding into her office, she found Wade with his elbows on his desk, his head resting in his hands.

"What's wrong?"

He snapped his head up. "Nothing. Just got my family settled in after convincing my father that I wasn't going to tackle the stage coach today but would be happy to do so tomorrow. And assuring my mother that she can stay in the casita until the nudists leave now that she knows they aren't Buddhists."

"Buddhists?" Even through her worry, she found the humor in that. "She really thought we were saying Buddhist resort the whole time?"

He nodded before leaning back in his chair and linking his hands behind his head.

Her gaze immediately went to his bare biceps and triceps, causing a zing of need to tighten her belly. Shaking off the thought, she strode to her desk. "I'll stop by and say hello as soon as I find my mother." She glanced at the clock, hesitant to wake Hunter up, especially since he was on tonight.

"Oh, I saw her take her dogs down the new desert trail walking path about twenty minutes ago."

She swallowed. "Did she see Ginger or Buddy?"

Wade sat forward again, his gaze alert. "I don't know. You didn't tell her yet?"

"No. I keep getting side tracked. I have to tell her right away." Turning away from her desk, she headed for the door.

"You want me to come with you?"

She gave him a quick smile. "No, this is a problem of my own making. I need to tackle it." She kept on down the hall then stopped and back-tracked. Sticking her head in the office, she grinned. "But if you'd like to go talk to Selma, make sure she's alright, and see if she still wants her job. I'm good with that."

Before he could respond, she headed down the hall again, her cowboy boots giving away exactly how fast she was walking.

She let Lacey know where she was headed as she walked by the reception desk then she was out the door. She waved to the guests by the pool and swallowed hard as she noticed Buddy and Ginger in the conversation pool.

Picking up her pace, she headed down the trail. It was late afternoon, so there wasn't a lot of activity beyond the pools thanks to the warmth of the day. It was in the high seventies and for their northern guests, quite balmy. For those who lived in the desert, it was refreshing.

She passed by the saguaro cacti, prickly pear patches and paloverde trees, all labeled per Lacey's research. Mesquite trees also had signs as well as the now bloomless wildflowers. When they had set about putting out the identification signs, they'd found jackrabbit scat and Lacey had insisted on a sign, but she refused. She had Chris scoop it up in a shovel and get rid of it.

The path wound upward before going down toward the small stream. It was two miles long, but she couldn't imagine her mom walking that far. Not seeing her ahead on the incline, Kendra started to jog. Again, that new worry started in her gut that her mom was hurt. Was that because she was at Poker Flat?

She reached the highest part of the path only to turn the bend to find her mom on a boulder just off the path a few yards down. "Mom."

Her mother looked up then away. Had she been crying? Shit. She'd only seen her mom cry three times in her life. The first time was when she realized Fred was cheating on her. The second time was at her first wedding, but she didn't think those were happy tears. The last time her mother cried was when she said goodbye to her as she took off on the poker circuit.

She started forward only to halt as Freckles and Scruffy ran onto the path and barked at her. Her heartrate went into overdrive as her palms started to sweat. Luckily, her mother held the leashes. She licked her lips, trying to moisten her suddenly dry mouth. "Mom, are you okay?"

"Of course. What's your problem?"

"Can you hold the dogs closer so I can come down?"

Her mother didn't move. "Why do you want to come down?"

Freak. Something was definitely wrong. "So we can talk."

"Go talk to your bosom buddies Ginger and Buddy. I hear they are part of the wedding party. Not sure why you wanted me to come. It's not like I'm important or anything."

Fuck. This was her fault. She'd been focused on Poker Flat instead of her wedding or her mom. "Of course, you're important. Why do you think I sent you an airline ticket and bought you that beautiful blue gown? You're the mother of the bride."

Her mom looked at her. "Damned right, I am. No red topped nudie can say that."

"No, she can't. Ginger is going to be the matron of honor. I think the bridesmaids are all wearing pale yellow."

"You think?"

She grimaced. "Lacey is my wedding planner. She's taking care of the details. She went with them to get their dresses, not me."

Her mother seemed to relax at that.

"Can you pull the dogs in so I can come closer?"

Her mom appeared to think about it for a minute, but then she clicked a button on the mechanism she had with the leashes and pulled the dogs closer. "Come on, sweeties. Big Kendra, owner of the Poker Flat nudie resort, is afraid of you."

That made it clear they hadn't cleared the air yet. She walked cautiously forward, still keeping her distance by a couple yards, just in case. "Mom, you'll look beautiful as Luke walks you down the aisle."

"Yeah, so, who's walking *you* down the aisle?"

She tensed. "I'm having Buddy walk me down."

"Of course, you are. You always liked them better than your own parents while you were growing up. If they hadn't been kicked out, I would have never seen you as a teenager."

Her mother wasn't far from the truth. "It's not that I liked them better than you. It's that I couldn't stand how Fred treated you. I've always loved you, mom. I've always liked you, too. It was Fred. He made being home hell."

"That's true. I started to hate it when he came home, too. I found myself wishing he'd get a new girlfriend just so I could have some peace, especially after your friends moved out of the park. I liked it when it was just us girls."

Kendra smiled. "I did, too. But why did you stay? He treated you like shit."

"And then some." Her mom sighed. "But what could I do? I couldn't provide for us without his income and that blasted trailer. I was stuck."

"What about after I got married to Eugene? Why didn't you leave then?"

"Where would I go? Like you, I'm an only child, so it wasn't as if I could go to family, and all my friends lived in the park. Besides, after a while, it was just easier to stay. The Devil you know versus the shit you don't."

She'd been guilty of that, too. Her ex had treated her like her big bust meant she was stupid, but it had been easier to let it slide in exchange for a nice roof over her head and an escape from her life in the trailer park. It wasn't until she sensed him moving on to better fish with equally big boobs that she found her backbone. "I understand that. But now you're here and you are my mother and I want everyone to see how proud I am of you."

Her mother laughed loudly. "Layin' it on a bit thick, aren't you? You made it clear before you married that you were ashamed of us."

"I know. I'm sorry. I just didn't understand why you let Fred walk all over you. But look at you now. You took in two lonely dogs." She glanced at them, happy to see them lying at her mom's feet. "And now you've left him. You're going to make it permanent with a divorce, too. I'm very proud of you."

Her mother's smirk turned into a genuine smile. "Yeah, that's true, because I had someplace to go."

"And I'm so glad you did." She gazed at her mom through new eyes, understanding her more than she had her entire life. The sun had started to set and the sky behind her mom was changing colors. It was a metaphor for both of them, except she would be changing again. She would marry a man who truly loved her, flaws and all.

Though she wouldn't admit it to anyone, she didn't believe it would actually happen. He was going to wake up and realize he could do so much better than her, and she wouldn't blame him a bit. He was too damn close to perfect to be saddled with her. If she was a stronger person, she let him off the hook, but a small part of her hoped he'd forget to take off his rose-colored glasses and stay with her.

"I guess it's okay that Ginger and Buddy are here. After all, you do need someone to walk you down the aisle."

At her mom's voice, she refocused. "Thanks, mom."

Her mother stood. "Well, these two have had plenty of rest from their walk. Better get them back so they can have dinner."

The two dogs immediately jumped to their feet and looked up at her mother, tails wagging.

Her heart started to race again and she took a few steps back.

"Kennie, you need to get over this fear."

She waved away her mom's comment and backed up some more. "I know. Maybe after the wedding. I'll be a bit more relaxed then."

Her mom sighed. "Fine. Go do what you have to do then because we're headed back."

She didn't need to be told twice. Turning around, she strode back up to the peak of the trail and around the corner. When she heard her mother's chuckle behind her, she grimaced but she didn't slow down. She had no problem being afraid of dogs until now. That was one fear she would rather never deal with.

As she came off the trailhead, she found Wade waiting for her.

"Are you ready for a private dinner?" He winked.

Happy to see him after the emotional minefield she'd just navigated, she took his hand in hers. "Yes, I am."

"And your mom?"

She looked him in the eye. "She's fine. We're both fine."

He squeezed her hand. "Good. That means I'll have your mind as well as your body all to myself for a while."

"Yes, you will." They headed back toward the main building, the pool and bar area quiet as guests were back at their casitas or in the dining room for dinner. She needed to find a way to focus on Wade more, just in case he did decide he would go through with marrying a former poker player and current workaholic from a trailer park. The question was, how was she going to do that?

~~~~~

Monday

Wade strode down the Old West town, the happiest he'd been
~~~~~

in days. Before the Ditzmans left on Saturday, they'd agreed it had been their fault that Mr. Ditzman was bit by the snake, and then the last Poker Flat guest left on Sunday.

Now his family could come out of hiding and they all could relax. That wasn't to say his mother hadn't ventured up to meet with Lacey the first day she arrived, but she'd hidden away in the staff room to confer with their wedding planner.

Even Kendra seemed a bit more relaxed once the final guest left and while she wasn't paying much more attention to the wedding details, she did seem to be more focused on him. Having her focus was like hitting the jackpot, especially in bed. They'd actually been able to go to bed together last night, which had been enjoyable for them both.

He'd even sent Chris to pick up Natasha for their line dance practice. With no guests to feed, she was able to come in much later. Tomorrow would be the first time they'd all get to practice together. His best man, Dale, his older brother Luke, and his younger brother Tanner would arrive later in the day. He just hoped Kendra didn't get up earlier than usual tomorrow and discover them all.

He unlocked the sliding barn door and strode into the saloon. Switching on the lights, he couldn't help but think there had to be something they could do with the space. He'd talk to Kendra about it.

Stepping back out onto the boardwalk, he caught site of Jorge across the way leading Ace into the corral. The day had the feeling of a holiday. It was beyond odd not to have guests at Poker Flat. Since the day they opened the doors, the place had guests.

As if on cue, the dust from a golf cart broke the horizon of the fork and headed toward him. Natasha was right on time as usual. It was hard to imagine she'd been fired for being late. Chris, on the other hand, had been fired for a completely different reason.

Wade had no use for homophobes. It seemed that Chris' roommate for now didn't either. He found it odd that Kane hadn't left for his own home by now, unless he really couldn't drive yet.

The golf cart came closer and it became clear someone else was on it. What the hell. The resort was closed. He jogged down the two steps to the packed dirt to meet them. No sooner had Chris stopped the cart then a man in a white cowboy hat, jeans, blue checked shirt and cowboy boots jumped off the back. He was tall, dark-haired and way too familiar.

"I'm here. The party can start, now."

Wade laughed. "Shit, Dale. I wasn't expecting you until this afternoon. I thought you were working."

As he hugged his long-time friend, excitement at the reality of his approaching wedding built. With his best man arriving, it suddenly felt real.

When they separated, Dale smirked. "I couldn't wait. I've got a great second in command at the office, and with my phone attached to my hip, I figured, what the heck. Besides, I wanted to show you how much more dance practice you'd need to catch up to me."

"Don't count on it. I may be pathetic at the waltz, but I can boot scoot with the best of them."

His friend laughed. "Good to hear it. I wouldn't want to show up the groom."

"Not happening my friend."

Dale looked around. "Wow, this place has really grown."

Again, that surge of pride filled his chest. "Kendra has done wonders, not to mention the excellent staff you've sent."

"Excellent? Are you kidding? I send her the people I can't get other clients to take."

"Well, they're thriving here."

Dale shook his head. "I'll never forget the day she came into my office and told me she only wanted workers who needed a second chance. I thought she was nuts. But it's worked for her for the most part."

Wade opened his arm toward the saloon and they walked up the steps. "It has. She's only had to fire a few. Rachel, our former waitress, was the last and that was over six months ago." He kept the Selma issue to himself. She'd been recruited directly by Kendra, so she didn't affect Dale's track record.

"Rachel? Oh yes, she was the one who had stolen cash from the register at her old job. Why was she fired from here? I thought your dining area didn't operate on cash."

"It doesn't, but we do have a charge to the room system, and she was changing the tip amounts, often by ten dollars. It wasn't until the third guest's bill had to be adjusted that Lacey figured out what was happening. We have no idea how many guests didn't even notice."

Dale shook his head as he entered the saloon then stopped. "This looks great. Do you have wild west shows for the guests, too? I've seen one over in Cave Creek where they have trick riding, shoot outs with a fake bank robbery and an all-out bar fight."

Wade chuckled. "No, we don't. Breaking glass isn't the best thing to have around nudists, if you know what I mean."

Dale nodded in understanding as Natasha came over to start the practice.

Wade scrutinized Dale as Natasha put them through their paces. His best friend was as good as he said and their practice went well. When they were done, he stopped Chris as he started down the boardwalk. "Hey, how's your house guest?"

The young man's face lit up. "He's doing great. He still can't move around a lot yet, but he can see now. His eyes aren't swollen anymore, but they look awful, all purple and yellow."

"Does he need a ride back to his house?"

Chris shook his head. "No. Hunter went with me to pick up Kane's car. I told Kane he can stay as long as he wants." Chris looked away. "Besides, I bring him Natasha's great meals and I made him breakfast yesterday. He's content to recover at my place."

He hoped Chris didn't have a crush on the man. By his own admission, Kane wasn't gay. "Okay. Keep me updated."

"I will."

As the masseuse stopped at the door to the Sheriff Office where he gave massages, Wade called out again. "Hey Chris, what are you doing? We have no guests today."

Chris didn't turn around. "I know. I just need to get a relaxation lotion for Kane. I'm hoping it will help the tight muscles around his broken ribs."

Wade wanted to question him further, but Dale grabbed his arm.

"Come on. I left my suitcase up in my car. I need to get it and then I want the full tour."

The inkling of unease about Kane dissipated as he focused on

Dale. "I'll be happy to. You haven't been here since the resort was first built, right?"

"Actually, before that the barn hadn't even been built. Your fiancé had a lot of problems negotiating the politics for permits for this place."

He grimaced as they settled in his golf cart. "I know. Occasionally, we still get vandals, but mostly they're young people sneaking out here on a dare. Hunter and Mac are excellent."

Dale chuckled. "I'm glad to hear you say that. This was my last hope for Hunter and I knew when Mac walked in that the only place she'd stand a chance was here. What you two are doing here is creating a haven for misfits and I have to tell you, I'm definitely the beneficiary."

Wade started them toward the dirt fork in the road. "I'm glad. I never thought returning that favor you did me back in college would have turned out so well. To tell you the truth I hadn't been looking forward to working here. Now, I couldn't imagine working anywhere else."

"Not even on that ranch you've dreamed about all your life?"

He thought back to his simple dream of owning a horse ranch. His imagination could have never conjured a Poker Flat. His dream had definitely changed. "Let's just say that I've come to the reality of what working and living at the same place is all about. Sure, I grew up on our ranch, but dad was in charge and that was family. That working ranch has morphed in my mind to a nice house in the middle of nowhere without even a garden to work on."

Dale turned thoughtful as they crossed the stream. "I know what you mean. Owning my own business has been a struggle, but like here, it's flourishing now. I'm sort of in that place of having accomplished my dream and now I don't know where to go from here."

He raised his right hand and wiggled his bare ring finger. "There's always marriage."

"Marriage. I don't even have time to ask a woman out."

He maneuvered around the last switchback before answering. "Sounds like we're both in need of a vacation."

Dale chuckled. "Somehow I don't think this time we'll be able to go together."

He didn't have a chance to answer because as they crested the ledge, he found cars pulling into the garage.

His friend patted him on the back as they pulled to a stop. "Looks like the gang's all here."

He stopped the golf cart. "Yes, a lot earlier than I expected. I better call Jorge and have him bring up the wagon."

"See, we're all excited for you. Any chance I can grab my stuff, take this cart and get checked-in before saying hello to everyone? My guess is you don't need me for this initial family reunion."

He watched as his family started piling out of the trucks and cars. "Yes. Go ahead." He handed Dale the key. "Lacey will be waiting for you."

"Great, I will see Miss Winters and settle in. Catch you later."

"Don't call her Miss Winters. It's Mrs. Hatcher now, but she prefers Lacey."

"Got it." Dale ducked behind a truck and moved toward his car.

Wade stepped out of the cart and frowned. Well shit. He'd

totally forgotten Dale used to have a crush on his little sister. Did he still have feelings for her?

"There's the man who got smart and decided to marry even smarter."

At his younger brother's words, he strode forward. As he gave Tanner a hug, he winked at his girlfriend. Soon he was greeting his older brother Luke and his younger sister Raine.

Luke appeared more like himself then he had the last time Wade had seen him almost six months ago. Raine looked great. As full of life as usual. After ribbing her about not bringing a date because she *always* had a boyfriend or friend or whatever they called it at her age, he piled everyone into the wagon. He sat next to Jorge on the front bench so he could watch his siblings' reactions to seeing Poker Flat for the first time. It was a moment he'd never be tired of experiencing.

Much like having Kendra in his life…forever.

CHAPTER NINE

Monday continued.

Kendra stood in the doorway drinking coffee as Lacey and her future mother-in-law discussed where to put the flower arrangements at the top of the aisle. She found the whole conversation boring yet the two were so excited, it was as if *they* were getting married.

Maybe there was something wrong with her. Shouldn't she be excited about all these little details? It was her wedding after all. But every time they asked her opinion, the image of the wedding planner from her first wedding rose in her mind.

The woman had been at least twenty years her senior and impeccably dressed. When the planner asked her a question, *if* she asked, she made the correct answer obvious. The few times Kendra had expressed her opinion, Eugene had sided with the wedding planner, citing what their guests would like as their first priority.

She was older now and could have a say in every detail of the wedding, but it just didn't seem that important. In a way, she wished she and Wade were already married. She was trying to ignore the whole wedding event, but it was a cloud over what should be the most important day of her life.

Maybe it was because she once believed that. Her first wedding had gone off beautifully, perfect. Everyone was happy, even herself. But after that, the marriage was demoralizing and the divorce painful. She didn't want that to happen again. Maybe if she stayed out of the plans and the excitement, her marriage to Wade would be the opposite. In her head, she knew that was illogical, but the knot in her stomach as the day approached just got tighter and tighter.

Last night, she'd woken in the middle of the night and eaten a hamburger bun she found in the cabinet just to give her stomach a distraction.

"What do you think, Kendra?" Lacey looked at her expectantly.

"About which thing?"

Her future mother-in-law chuckled. "I know it's a lot of details. We were wondering if you were okay if the bows at the end of the rows of chairs were different from the ones on the stage coach."

She took a sip of coffee to hide her disinterest. "I think that's fine."

"I told you, Lacey. Kendra's just daydreaming about my son and I can't blame her." As Wade's mom went back to the pad of paper in front of her, Lacey gave her a quizzical look.

She gave a faint smile, nodded, then slipped away. She meandered down the hallway and toward the Great Room. It wasn't just the wedding. With the resort closed, there wasn't as much to do. She'd been working for weeks to be ready for it to reopen after the wedding, so now she felt rudderless.

Wade was busy with his family and friends. Her friends were her staff. It was odd that they were paying them to work, but they were also in the wedding. When did her life become only work?

The answer was obvious. The day she signed the divorce papers. Why was she still reacting to that? Why couldn't she take control of her life without that baggage weighing her down?

She turned as the side door to the outside opened.

"There you are, Kennie. I ran into that handsome hunk of yours and he said I'd find you here. He said his mom has been here for a few days already."

As her mom strode forward in a rainbow tee-shirt and yellow leggings, she grinned. "Yes, she's here, but she was hiding out in her casita because she thought we ran a Buddhist resort, not a nudist resort."

Her mom laughed loud, easily heard in the staff room, but she didn't care. That's who her mom was.

"That's hilarious. See, I told you to explain it as a nudie resort. Then there'd be no doubt." Her mom paused, and a devilish look entered her eyes. "Unless people mistook it for a booty resort, then they'd think it was a freakin' whorehouse." Again, her mom laughed loudly.

"You've been talking to Adrianna, haven't you?"

Her mom grinned. "You bet. You can learn a lot from that hot *chica*. Did you know she's had sex with—"

"I thought I heard people out here." Mrs. Johnson stood across the room, a polite smile on her face.

Happy the woman interrupted before she heard things she didn't want to know, Kendra motioned to her mom. "Mom, this is Wade's mother, Karen Johnson."

"Well, look at you, all pretty as a peach. How are you?" Her mom walked forward, her hand extended.

Wade's mom didn't seem to know what to do, so she shook hands.

"I was just telling Kennie what a hunk of a man your son is. Of course, my girl isn't too shabby either."

Karen looked at her then back at her mom.

"I know, the resemblance is uncanny isn't it? It's like we're sisters."

At her mother's words, she bit her lip to keep from laughing as Wade's mom struggled to keep her smile, but she finally cracked, a soft chuckle emanating from her. "Yes, it is. You must be very proud of what she's created here."

"You mean a first-class nudie resort? You bet. What was your name again?"

Mrs. Johnson's brows rose before she gave a genuine smile. "My name is Karen."

"I'm Donna."

"Donna, would you like to help Lacey and I with a few details? We could use your input."

Her mom looked over at her. "Hmmm, what a nice offer."

She shrugged. "I'm leaving it all to Lacey, so whatever you want, go for it."

Her mother made a fist and brought her elbow down to her waist. "Yes!" She turned to Karen. "Let's see what we can do to make this wedding interesting."

Kendra opened her mouth to rein her mother in, but then closed it as the two women walked off together. Maybe her mother's additions would keep the wedding more real. Besides, she'd had no say in the last one. As the mother of the bride, she *should* have input.

At a loss for what to do, she decided it was time to find Wade. Maybe they could go riding…or something.

~~~~~

Monday night.

Swearing sounded on the other side of her office door warning her people were just outside. The door opened and Mac walked in with her grip on a man.

As he turned to face her, Kendra rose. "Fred? What the hell are you doing here?" He was the last person she'd expected to show up. He hadn't changed at all. He was still short and pudgy, with a face like a dough boy and thick wavy brown hair that supposedly the ladies loved.

"Kendra. Finally. Someone who's reasonable. Tell this giant I have a right to see my wife."

Freak, wrong words to spew, Fred. She moved her gaze to Mac, whose eyes had darkened as they narrowed at Fred, the woman's whole body stiff. "Mac, let him go and step back."

Part of her wanted Mac to ignore her and give Fred the beating he'd deserved his whole life, but the other part of her didn't want Mac to face the repercussions, so she kept her tone stern. "Mac."

Finally, Mac released her hold and took two steps back, but her eyes didn't leave Fred for an instant.

"Fred, how the hell did you get here? I know you'd never spend the money on a plane ticket and mom took your only car."
~~~~~

"Yeah, that bitch stole my car."

She glanced at Mac to make sure she didn't move. She remained where she was, her focus lasered on Fred.

"That doesn't answer my question."

Fred blew her a kiss. "You sent me a plane ticket."

The smell of alcohol on his breath was so normal that she almost didn't notice it, but with his breath wafting over to her, she remembered it all too clearly. "No, I sent *mom* a plane ticket."

He shrugged. "I have a very good friend who works for the airline. She was able to switch it to my name. Thank you, by the way, for inviting me to your wedding. Now if you don't mind, I want to see my wife."

His tone had risen and Mac moved a step closer.

"Mac, he's not worth it."

That seemed to get through to her. She stepped back and her shoulders relaxed a bit.

"Mom doesn't want to see you. She's left you for good. She's filed for divorce. In fact, if you hadn't left, you probably would have the papers in hand right now." That was a bit far from the truth, since her mom didn't even have an appointment until next week, but Fred didn't need to know that. He was a lying bastard. She could be, too, to him.

"A divorce? She can't divorce me! How's she gonna live? Get a job?" He laughed, the sound guttural and nasty ending in a cough. "She can't divorce me. She needs me to keep a roof over her head."

What an asshole. He thought he had a live-in slave with her mother. Time for a reality check. "Actually, she doesn't. I'll take care of her until she can get on her feet." And damn if she didn't suddenly feel proud that she could do that.

"Nice try, but I know she's got them stinking dogs and there's no way in hell you'd have dogs in your house."

She crossed her arms, enjoying her opportunity to prove how powerless he was after all the years he made her mother feel that way. "Obviously, you didn't notice in the dark, but there's more than one residence on this property and mom has her own. She doesn't have to share with anyone, and never again with a lazy, selfish bastard like you."

Fred paused at that before his brow lowered. He looked mean, but as she'd discovered early in her life, he was all bark and no bite. "You can't talk to your father like that."

She laughed. She couldn't help it. Obviously, Fred's brain was the size of a pea. No wonder he thought more with his dick than his head. "Mac, where'd you find him?"

"He must have come while I was checking the staff casitas. By the time I finished my rounds by the stables, he was past the fork and headed for the bar."

"Yeah, I heard a party going on over there. Figured I could find someone to tell me where Donna was."

She glanced at the clock. She'd been gone way over the ten minutes she'd told Wade. She needed to get back and Fred needed to be gone. She turned her attention to Mac. "Escort him off the property."

"What? You're not going to offer me a place to stay? Where am I supposed to go? It took me all day to get a ride up here. It's not like I have a car."

And that was the solution to their problem. She looked at

her security guard, who towered over Fred. It made her think of a fantasy movie she saw once when a mythical Amazon held a scared troll over a cliff. "Do you still have mom's keys?"

"Yes." Mac patted her lightweight sweats.

"And is all of mom's things out of the car now?"

Mac nodded.

"Then give him the keys and show him where the car is and make sure he leaves." She opened her top drawer and pulled out the keys to Wade's truck. Her colt slid into view with the force of her pull. She threw the keys to Mac. "Follow him to be sure he makes it to the Carefree Highway." She reached down and pulled out the gun. "You can take this to make sure he doesn't give you any trouble." She knew he wouldn't, but she needed him to know how serious she was.

Mac shook her head. "I don't need that. I didn't need it with the last man I killed. Besides it doesn't look good for an ex-con to have a gun."

Fred snapped his head around to look at Mac. When he finally looked at Kendra again, his skin had paled considerably. "No need for violence. I know when I'm not wanted."

"Good." She made a show of putting the colt back in its place and closing the drawer. "Here in Arizona, we shoot first and ask questions later, so you better not show up sneaking around my property again."

Already forgetting Mac's presence. Fred scowled and took a step in her direction, his posture menacing. "You think you're some kind of big shot now, don't you?"

She didn't move a muscle, disgusted with the pathetic man her mother had married. "Mac, get him out of here."

As Mac grabbed hold of Fred, he started cursing all over again. After she hauled him out the door, Kendra dropped her head. The man had killed so many brain cells with alcohol, there was a good chance he wouldn't remember anything they'd said. She'd have to let Mac know that and alert Hunter.

Lifting her head, she turned off her computer and strode to the door. It opened before she could grab the handle.

Wade stood there, his brow furrowed. "Everything okay in here? I just saw Mac walking a man away. Did we have another trespasser?"

She nodded. "Yeah, my biological father."

Wade's eyes widened. "You had him escorted off the property?" His incredulity reminded her that he didn't truly understand her relationship with Fred.

"Yes, and I told him not to come back. But I don't think that's going to work."

"Are you sure that's the right way to handle it. You're his only daughter. Maybe he wants to be a part of your wedding."

She snorted. "He only mentioned the wedding because he used mom's plane ticket. He just wanted mom back and his car. He's getting one of those. Trust me. This is how he needs to be handled."

Wade studied her then nodded. "I do trust you."

The tension in her shoulders since seeing Fred walk through the door finally released. "Thank you."

He wrapped one arm around her waist and led her into the hall. "Are you ready to face the jovial masses?"

She took a deep breath. "I am, but…"

"But what? Tell me."

She looked into his warm brown eyes and almost forgot

what she was going to say. She felt as if she'd been dealt four aces and a king. "Do you think we could find some time to be alone tomorrow? Maybe go for a ride?"

His smile was so wide, she could almost feel his answer before he said a word. "Yes. To our special spot on the creek."

She nodded, her whole body finally relaxing. "There's a certain shelf above the water I'd like to visit."

He laughed and pulled her along the hall. "Definitely, a well-deserved treat after having to hang out with my family."

She stopped their forward progress. "Oh, no. I love your family. I just want to take advantage of the resort being closed to be with you."

He looked into her eyes with so much love that her own heart swelled. "I knew there was a reason I loved you." He lowered his lips to show her in a gentle kiss that he meant every word.

She sighed, finally finding some contentment as they walked through the Great Room and out to the bar where a cheer went up at their return.

~~~~~

Tuesday

Kendra crossed her fingers as Wade knocked on Selma's door. After three days without her leaving her casita with all the curtains and blinds drawn, they couldn't wait any longer. They had both tried to get her to open the door, but she hadn't responded.

Kendra listened intently, hoping they'd hear something, footsteps, a moan, anything.
~~~~~

Finally, Wade shook his head. "We have to go in."

Removing her master key from the loop on her jeans, she inserted it into the lock and slowly opened the door, half expecting an object to come flying at her head.

There were no lights on as they stepped into the open concept main living area, but the daylight seeped in between the blind slats to reveal the contents of the room.

"Wow." Wade's whispered word echoed her own thought.

Stuffing from couch cushions was scattered about like a mountain lion had shredded them. Broken vases, picture frames and lamps were scattered across the space. Every piece of furniture was overturned.

Worry turned to real fear. Had Selma hurt herself?

Wade put his hand on her shoulder as if he knew what she'd been thinking. Either that or his thoughts had gone in the same direction. "Selma?" His deep voice carried throughout the space.

"*Que?*"

Relief washed through her at the sound of Selma's voice. "Selma, can we talk to you?"

"*Madre dios*, there's no privacy at this place anymore."

The door to Selma's bedroom opened and she shuffled out. She wore a pair of jeans and a colorful short sleeved top. She looked perfectly fine. "What do you want to talk about?"

Wade frowned as he opened his arm to encompass the room. "How about this for starters?"

Selma waved her hand aside. "That's my temper. When I'm done. I'll clean it up."

They looked at each other. Done? She had to ask. "Done with what?"

Their cook moved into her galley kitchen and pulled out a jug of orange juice and set it on the counter before looking at them. "With your wedding present. I want to finish it before I leave."

Kendra stepped carefully as she moved toward the counter that separated the kitchen area from the living area. "Where are you going?"

Selma shrugged. "I don't know. But I can't stay here."

Wade joined her. "Why?"

She pointed. "She fired me."

"I didn't fire you." She frowned. "At least not yet. You know I always give people a second chance."

Selma stopped pouring her orange juice and stared. "But you hire a new cook."

Now how did she know that if she had stayed in her casita the last three days, unless… "Selma, have you been spying on us?"

The older woman looked away and finished pouring her glass of juice. "You want some?"

Wade turned toward her and gestured toward Selma. "That was a yes."

She nodded. Selma had a habit of avoiding admitting anything. Here they thought she'd been starving to death in her casita or had done herself damage and she was lurking about the resort. That's why they didn't hear anything when they knocked. "I want to know why you destroyed my kitchen and dining room on Friday, and be sure to tell the truth in English or you *will* be fired."

Selma, who had opened her mouth to answer, closed it. Instead she took a sip of her juice. When she put her glass down, she looked first to Wade. She finally shifted her gaze to meet hers straight on. "Jorge. He break my heart."

"I spoke to Jorge. He said he asked you to dinner, gave you flowers, and even fixed your window, but you weren't interested."

Selma took another sip of juice, clearly avoiding eye contact. "I didn't want him to think me easy conquest. Mama say, easy for sex, hard for life. I don't want just sex. I know how men treat women for sex."

Kendra looked at Wade, not sure how to answer that. Selma had run a brothel in Nevada. She'd probably seen a lot.

"Do you like Jorge that much?" Wade leaned his elbows on the counter next to her.

Selma silently nodded.

"He thinks you're crazy now."

Their cook's head snapped up. "I'm not crazy."

Kendra pointedly looked around the room. "Really?"

Selma didn't say anything.

Kendra looked at Wade. "So what should we do with her?"

"She owes us a lot of money for broken dishware in the main building, plus the wall in the kitchen will need to be repaired and there were at least three pots that need to be replaced, according to Natasha."

"The dancer?" Selma's exclamation had them both looking at her. "What she know about cooking? She nothing but skin and bones. She don't even fucking eat enough."

"Yes, Natasha. She was raised helping her mother cook." He gave Selma a piercing look. "And she doesn't throw dishes."

Kendra ignored Selma's outburst. "Are you saying we should let Selma keep her job and garnish her wages to pay for the damage?"

Wade nodded.

"But what about her temper? Can we trust her again?"

Wade looked at Selma. "If she does it again, then we fire her. Just like you did with Rachel."

The look on Selma's face at the chance to keep her job was heartbreaking, but Kendra stayed firm. "I think she needs to do more than just resume her duties."

Before Wade could answer, Selma jumped in. "What?"

"You need to apologize to my mother and to Jorge."

Selma's eyes widened then she shook her head.

Wade stood at that. "Very well. Then you can pack your bags and be gone by sunset."

"What? No."

Kendra moved to stand next to Wade. "Yes."

The older woman looked away, her fingers turning the juice glass as if she didn't realize what she did. "Fine. I apologize."

Kendra responded immediately. "Today."

As if caught in her plan, Selma's shoulders sagged, and she nodded. "*Hoy.*"

Wade smiled. "Good. That gives you today to clean this up and talk to Donna and Jorge. We'll see you bright and early tomorrow morning."

Selma nodded, her mind obviously still trying to come up with a way out of the apology.

They walked around the debris to get to the door. As Wade opened it, Kendra turned back. "Today."

Selma frowned and waved them out. Once outside, they heard the door lock behind them. Wade chuckled. "You do know how to pick your staff."

She grinned. "Thank you. I do think I do an exceptional job with that. After all, I chose you."

Laughing, he led her to the golf cart they'd taken from their house. Being together during the day, but not in the office, was a new experience. One she was enjoying.

As he drove them to the main building, she remembered their bet. "I was right."

"About what?"

"About Selma being sweet on Jorge. That means I win the bet." She was bursting with anticipation.

"You're right, you did win. I just wish it wasn't at such an expense financially or emotionally. Do you think Jorge will accept her apology?"

"I don't know. He seemed pretty freaked out about her actions. Would you want to start a relationship with a woman who had done that?"

He stopped the golf cart at the main building and looked at her. "You mean would I ask a woman to marry me who was ready to kill a man?"

At his reminder of her own loss of control shortly after opening the resort, she closed her lips tight. Who knew? Maybe Jorge would be interested after all.

They were walking toward the main building when Dale and Tanner came out. Dale opened his arms wide. "There you are. We were looking for you."

"You found me."

Tanner grabbed him by the arm. "And now you're coming with us."

Wade resisted, looking at her in confusion. They were about to get a picnic lunch and go for their ride. "Whoa, where am I supposed to be going?"

Dale grabbed his other arm. "To your bachelor party."

"What? I thought those happened at night and involved a stripper." He tried to resist, but the two men started to pull him toward a golf cart.

Dale laughed. "How boring would that be to a man who sees naked women every day? Nope, thanks to Lacey, we're going for a trail ride at Last Chance and then we're going to roast marshmallows over a campfire while we roast you and sleep out under the stars." His best man winked at Kendra.

Wade mouthed the word "sorry" to her, but she smiled and waved him off. It was tradition after all.

Wade still resisted. "Who else is going? I'm not sure I'll be safe out there with you two."

Tanner chuckled. "Oh, don't worry. Dad, Luke, Lowell, Jorge, Chris, Hunter, and Buddy are all going. We're going to make sure we rehash every embarrassing moment of your life, big brother."

He groaned as he let them push him down into the seat. "If we're not back tomorrow, call detective Anderson and report me as a missing person."

Kendra laughed and waved as they took him down the dirt road. Though she was disappointed, she was happy for him. That's what a Bachelor party should be, not three women in bed for the entire night, like her ex had. He claimed he wore a condom, but she got tested after their honeymoon only to discover she had syphilis and needed to be treated, the asshole.

At least he'd have something to do for the next twenty-four hours. Now to figure out what she should do. She could always go into her office and review the fall marketing plans. After a full day off, she already didn't want to do that. Maybe she should find her mom or Lacey and see if she needed to do anything for the wedding. After all, it was *her* wedding. Turning, she strode to the dark glass doors and pulled one open.

"Surprise!!!"

She halted in her tracks as the all the women left on the resort stood there smiling and laughing. Ginger and her mom grabbed each of her hands and pulled her toward the Great Room. "What's this?"

Ginger squeezed her hand. "It's your bridal shower, sweetie."

Her bridal shower? What could they possibly give her that she didn't already have?

CHAPTER TEN

Wednesday

Wade headed straight for his office. He'd bet a thousand dollars he'd find Kendra behind her desk working. He smelled like smoke and horse, but he wanted to see her before he showered.

It was probably the best bachelor party he could have asked for. The laughter was constant, mostly at his expense, and the whiskey flowed. He didn't envy his brother Luke who not only had too much, but said too much, too, revealing more than he'd want known, if he remembered any of it.

Striding past the front desk, he slowed. Not having someone there greeting guests was strange. Picking up his pace, his boots echoing in the hall, he finally reached the closed door. Opening it, he smiled.

No one was there. What the hell? It was mid-afternoon, where else would Kendra be? Her mom's? His mom's? With Lacey? So much for his surprise entrance. Good thing he didn't bet anyone.

Closing the door, he was headed back out when movement to

his left caught his attention. Looking out the side windows of the Great Room, he saw Adriana serving a beer to Kendra. He took a double-take and strode closer. Holy shit! It was Kendra in a bikini! He'd never seen her in a bikini before. She rocked the simple tan bathing suit with white trim. The thought of other men seeing her like that cooled his ardor immediately.

Scanning down her body, he was surprised to see she was barefoot, water dripping from her feet.

She'd taken off her cowboy boots! The women must have convinced her that her leg was no big deal. He was excited in a whole new way. Quickly, he pulled off his boots and headed for the side door. Once outside, he came up on her from behind, wrapping his arms around her, grubby sleeves and all. "Hey, beautiful."

"Ack! Wade you stink!"

He laughed. "Nice way to greet your fiancé." He kissed her on the lips, loving the feel of them against his own.

She pulled her head away. "You need a shower or something."

He winked at Adriana before he pulled Kendra off the stool and toward the pool.

"What are you doing? Wade, you're the one who needs a shower, not me."

"You said *or something*." With those words, he dipped his head to drop his hat on the pool deck then pulled Kendra into the pool, both of them falling in together.

"Woo! Woot!" The cheers as they came up made him smile.

"Now that's a welcome home." He recognized Donna's voice as he held his still struggling fiancé.

"Wade, you're crazy?"

He nodded. "Yup, crazy for you." He kissed her and felt her

silent chuckle reverberate through her. When he breached her lips with his tongue, she wrapped her arms around his neck.

As she started to moan in his arms, he broke off the kiss. "I missed you."

She smiled. "I missed you, too."

"Anything important happen while I was gone?"

"Yes and no."

He raised his brows at that. "What does that mean?"

"It means yes, I received some interesting gifts at my bridal shower, and no, in that I nixed the head table for the wedding party and have it set with just you, me, your parents and my mom."

"That's perfect."

Her smile faltered. "I don't know about that. I just wanted mom to feel special."

"It's your wedding and you should do what you want."

She cocked her head at him. "And what do you want?"

Her question caught him off guard. A flippant response came to him, but the serious look in her blue gaze had him rethinking it. "I just want to have you for my wife."

"That's it? That's not much."

He lost his smile at that. "It's the world."

She studied him as if she thought he was joking.

"Kendra, you're far more than I ever expected to have in a wife. You're my partner, equal in everything. A man couldn't ask for more."

"I don't know why you see so much in me, but don't stop seeing it. Okay?"

The blatant insecurity of her statement had his arms tightening without thought. "Never."

She still didn't look completely convinced, so he cradled her head and showed her with his kiss.

"Wade Johnson, what are you doing in that pool with all your clothes on?"

His mother's voice came from behind him. He broke the kiss to answer her though he gave Kendra a wink. "What does it look like I'm doing?" Not waiting for an answer, he kissed her, the woman he loved, until she melted in his arms.

~~~~~

Kendra couldn't help her excitement as she stroked Sundancer and Ace. Jorge had saddled the horses for them and Wade was on his way. She was looking forward to the ride they'd planned on yesterday. She knew it was silly since they lived together, but they had so little time alone during the day to talk about anything besides Poker Flat and most recently the wedding. A ride into the desert where the cell phones couldn't reach them was exactly what she wanted.

Wade's words earlier in the pool had found their way to her heart and she wanted to tell him that she didn't doubt him. She was done with baggage. Baggage from her failed marriage. Baggage from her childhood, like her stupid leg scars. At the shower when her mother let slip about the coyote event and what an ass her father had been, the women had insisted on seeing her leg.

She'd flatly refused until Mac threatened to hold her down while Adriana took off her boot. With no choice, she's removed her boot and sock, expecting gasps or complete silence. Instead, they all started talking at once, telling her how it wasn't that bad and
~~~~~

about others they'd seen with worse deformities. A couple of them actually showed off their own scars. By the time everyone had their say, she was laughing so hard, her eyes teared up.

Last night, alone in her house, she'd really looked at her leg. Over the years, her skin had changed and the scars really weren't as bad as she remembered them. She had avoided looking at them for so long, even when showering, that she hadn't seen them for what they were, a faded memory.

The tight knot in her belly was slowly unraveling, and she had her family and friends to thank for that, but most of all, she had Wade.

She patted Ace then strolled into the barn to see what the other horses were doing.

"There you are."

At the sound of that voice, she spun to find Fred walking into the barn. Fury as strong as her happiness and maybe because of it, filled her. She lowered her brows as her blood surged. "I told you to get off my property. If I remember correctly I had you escorted off."

"Yeah, well that felon isn't here to do your dirty work, is she? You only have security at night. Yeah, I've been watching." He lifted a bottle of cheap bourbon up to his lips and drank.

A shudder ran through at the idea of Fred as a Peeping Tom, but it would make sense. Thankfully, her guests had already left. "I don't care what you've been doing. If you don't leave right now, I'll call the sheriff." She pulled her phone from her back pocket, her hand shaking with her fury.

He walked farther into the barn and sat on one of Jorge's lawn chairs pushed against the side of the tack room. "Go ahead, call. I'll be happy to tell them about your criminal."

That was all he had? Her brain started to focus with intense detail. The man was slipping. "She's not a criminal. She did her time. Now leave."

"What's wrong, darling daughter? Just can't call the cops on your dear father? Good, because I've come to walk you down the aisle tomorrow. That's my right."

Walk her…there was no way in hell she'd allow him *near* her wedding. Her heart raced at the gall of it. This was the man who couldn't afford to buy new school clothes, but spent money buying women drinks at the local bars. It was bad enough she was from a poor trailer park, but then when her chest got big, the clothes made it worse.

Here she'd thought she'd rid herself of baggage and it was staring her in the face. Her hand tightened around her phone of its own accord, the urge to throw it at him hard to resist. "You have no rights. You lost them the first time you slept around on mom."

He laughed. "Oh, I'd been doing that way before you were born. You weren't even supposed to be here. Your mother was on the pill."

Did he really think she'd didn't know every detail of his crimes against her mother? "I know the whole sordid story. About how you used the money she needed for her birth control to buy another bottle of booze. The laugh was on you, wasn't it? You were forced to pay to feed and house both of us."

He jumped up at that and gestured toward her with his bottle. "Damn right I did and that gives me rights." He spit on the barn floor. "Just what I needed, my bitch having a bitch. I thought I finally had it made when you married rich, but no, you couldn't throw some cash my way." He snarled. "You kept it to your fucking self. Not this time. I deserve to live here more than your mother." He squinted at her. "You – owe - me."

The absurdity of his thought process stunned her. He didn't give a shit about anything but his liquor and pussy. She took a step forward, trying to resist the urge to pummel him. "I don't owe you squat."

"Fuck that! You owe me for putting a roof over your head and feeding that fucking mouth of yours! You owe me your life! I'm your father, you fucking cunt!"

His insults toward her didn't faze her. She'd heard them hurled her way her entire life, but his self-absorption after all he'd put her through was too much. She stepped closer and pointed her finger at him, wanting more than anything to punch him. "Just because you stuck your pathetic dick inside my mother and squirted out some sperm doesn't make you my father!"

Before Fred could respond, she heard the crunch of cowboy boots on the dirt outside. Shit. She didn't want Wade involved in this.

"What's going on in here?" He loomed large in the doorway.

Fred pointed at her, his tone growing whiney. "She has no right to treat me like this. I'm her father."

"Wade, just give me few minutes. I need to finish this conversation so he understands." She nodded toward Fred, her breathing heavy as she tried to control her voice with Wade.

"No. I'm not leaving you alone with him."

Of course he wouldn't because he always stood by her. She tried one more time, not sure he needed to see exactly how low her beginnings really were. "He's not a threat. We just have some unfinished business that has finally come to a head."

Wade shook his head. "I know. But this man can inflict pain with words. I can't let that happen."

Her anger calmed in the face of his steadfastness. That she'd known what his answer would be before she'd asked just proved how in tune they were. She'd always had to fight her own battles, even against the man who thought he was a father. If Wade wanted to take care of this one for her, she was more than willing to let him. She glanced at Fred, who was grinning at her as if he thought he'd won.

"You know what? We're done. He's not worth any more of my time." She threw her hand to the side toward Fred. "If you'd like to escort him off the property for me, I'm good with that. I have a horse waiting for me."

Striding past Fred, she grabbed the whiskey bottle from his hand. "I always hated you. Now I could care less if you live or die." When she reached the dirt outside, she slammed the bottle to the ground and strode to Sundancer.

Untying the reins, she hopped on his back and kicked him into a gallop. She didn't care where they went, just away from the man she despised. She was done with him.

"I knew I liked you." Kendra's father's words penetrated Wade's surprise that Kendra had so quickly handed Fred over to him. That wasn't like her.

"You understand how these women are. She shouldn't be treating me like that. What is it that makes women such bitch—"

Wade crossed the space between them in an instant, his hand encircling the short, chubby man's neck. "You listen very carefully, Fred. You're going to be leaving here right now. If you return, I will be happy to bury your corpse out in the desert somewhere after my security team deals with you. Do you understand?"

Fred nodded his head, his face bright red.

"Good." He let go of the man's neck and grabbed him by the collar of his dirty shirt. Walking him out of the barn, he forced him into the golf cart Kendra had left behind. He wanted to ride after her but she'd left him the responsibility of getting rid of Fred. His concern was she was still a novice rider.

"Sure you don't want to run after her? Makeup fucking is hard and quick. None of that *make me wet,* shit."

Wade smacked the man on the back of his head.

"Ow!"

He needed to dump this piece of garbage. "Shut up." Decision made, he drove him up to the garage. Without a word, he walked Fred to his car.

Once the man unlocked his door and sat, Wade kept it from closing. "Are we clear?"

"Fuck you." Fred spit, but it fell far short of its mark.

He slammed the door and stepped away from the vehicle. Though Kendra believed her father wasn't dangerous, he wasn't as sure. Any person pushed into a corner could be dangerous, even himself.

Fred started the car and peeled out, sending a cloud of dust in the direction of the garage.

Wade watched until the car was out of sight. He didn't trust Fred as far as he could throw the man. He'd alert both Hunter and Mac that he might come back. If he'd let Kendra have it out with Fred, would that have that ended it for good?

He wouldn't apologize for protecting her. Fred was an

unknown to him. It had been hard staying out of it when Selma held a knife and iron pan. It was impossible with Fred, even if all he had was a bottle.

As he drove back down the ravine, the lights inside the main building showed his family and friends in the Great Room. In contrast, above the ravine, the sun was just starting to set.

He had to find Kendra before dark. He pushed the cart to its fastest and raced toward the barn, the shadows taking over everything. Jumping out, he untied Ace and mounted. "Come on, boy, we need to find the other half of my heart."

Kendra let Sundancer wander wherever he wanted, too lost in thought to pay attention. How had she gone from being the most stoic person on the resort to riding an emotional rollercoaster?

What would Wade think of Fred? How much had he heard? Just seeing Fred sent her back two decades, bringing her right back to when she was a younger girl. Even her language regressed.

Pissed at herself for letting the lowlife get to her, she brought Sundancer to a halt. Dismounting, she dropped the reins and looked around. She didn't recognize the area, but she was on some kind of trail.

Seeing the stream, she moved toward it. She crouched down and splashed the cold water on her face. The coolness felt good and she splashed her face again. Standing, she pulled her shirt out of her jeans and wiped her face.

How did she get to be the lucky one with all the baggage? Wade didn't have any at all. Even talking to his mother and siblings made it sound like he led a charmed life.

Maybe instead of crushing her past into submission, she

needed to just let it go. Fred didn't get it and he never would. She was wasting her breath trying to make him see what an ass he was. She should have realized that sooner. He wasn't so much the problem as the catalyst for the rest of her issues.

But she'd overcome those, hadn't she? She felt better about her body image, her mother, and even her origins. Her ex had been another source of her problems, but he'd probably forgotten about her, yet she was hyped up over her whole wedding because of him. Wade was not Eugene. They were opposites.

Eugene had used her to pursue his dream. Wade had given up his dreams of owning a ranch to be part of hers. It didn't get any more opposite than that. So why was she still nervous about the actual wedding? If she was so worried about it being perfect like her last one, she should have planned it. But when Lacey offered to take charge, her eyes alight with her excitement, she couldn't refuse.

Kendra stared at the Palo Verde tree across the stream, its green branches now appearing gray as the sun set over the desert floor above her. The sun would rise and fall no matter how much she worried about things. What had all her worrying done for her anyway? Nothing. No, worse than that, she'd made her life worse. She needed to allow events to happen as they would. She had to trust in her family, friends and staff.

Easier said than done, but she could try.

She needed to trust in Wade, too. No, she didn't *need* to, she *did*. Her confidence in their ability to handle whatever was thrown at them was solid, she just hadn't realized it. She wanted to smack herself in the forehead. Sometimes, she could be so blind. She had to go back and tell him, everything.

Turning around to find Sundancer, she froze.

A lone coyote stared at her and bared its teeth, a low rumbling sound emanating from its throat.

Panic flew up her spine and she was suddenly three-years-old again, a coyote's teeth sinking into her leg. The pain sliced through her psyche, stopping her heart. She forced the memory away, blinking as the white teeth of the animal before her came into focus. Fuck that. She was done with being afraid.

"Get out of here!" She stepped toward the coyote who spun and sprinted a few yards away.

"I said get!" The coyote ran a few more yards then sat on its haunches and lifted its head, a lonely howl coming from it.

No way was she dealing with a pack of them. Adrenaline suffused her limbs and she started to run, waving her arms. "Go. Get out of here or I'll come back with my Smith and Wesson and end your miserable life!"

The coyote bounded off in front of her as she ran after it. When she couldn't see it anymore, she stopped and bent over, taking deep breaths.

She did it. She did it! She wanted to yell to the world.

Standing up, she scanned the darkening landscape in triumph. Another piece of baggage thrown away. If she could chase off a coyote, she could certainly handle a perfect wedding.

"Kendra!"

At the sound of Wade's yell, she turned, her success turning to joy and excitement. "Over here!" She felt her eyes welling up again, but this time with happiness. Running down the incline she'd conquered to make the coyote leave, she skidded to a halt at the bottom.

"Where are you!" From the sound of his voice, Wade was worried.

She was beyond lucky to have him. "I'm down the trail!" She looked around for Sundancer but didn't see him. It had grown dark at the bottom of the ravine. "I'm near the stream." She started walking toward where she heard Wade.

As she came around an outcropping, she saw him, or rather his white hat and the pale shapes of two horses. Too thrilled he'd come for her, she ran toward him and jumped into his arms.

He held her tight for a moment, before pushing her back to look at her. "Are you alright?"

"I'm better now. You mean more to me than any of my past. If I ever do or say something stupid again, you remind me of the coyote."

He chuckled. "I can't say I understand half of what you're saying, but I'm glad you're unharmed."

She looked up into his eyes. "I'm better than unharmed." Without explanation, she kissed him, showing him exactly how fine she was.

Wade pulled away just as she was ready to take off his clothes and make love right there on the trail.

She groaned.

"You make me want to take you right now, but if you want to make our rehearsal dinner, we should probably get back. It's your call."

Kendra gave it serious thought. She wanted to be alone with him, but they'd have tonight. In the meantime, their family and friends were gathered on their resort to share their celebration. "As much as I want you all to myself, we should probably go."

"I agree." He helped her to mount and handed her the reins. "I hope you know that I knew you could handle Fred, but I can't help my protective instincts when it comes to you. I'll probably do the same thing again and again."

She cupped his cheek as he looked up to her. "I know. I'm counting on it. And if I ever get mad about that, you'll just have to forgive me."

"Deal."

She laughed, her happiness needing to come out somehow. Now she looked forward to her wedding. Her past was where it should be and only the future mattered now. As Sundancer and Ace walked along the dark trail, she contemplated exactly how to give Wade his wedding present, a big part of their future.

~~~~~

Thursday – Wedding Day

"Lacey, stop. Everything's going to go fine, and will you put down that damn clipboard." Kendra spoke to Lacey in the reflection of the mirror in the Old West Saloon. Lacey had commandeered it for the women in the bridal party to get ready.

Lacey looked over her shoulder. "In a minute. Just hold still while Adriana secures your veil. You don't want it to be crooked."

Actually, she wouldn't mind that in the least, but she couldn't share that with Lacey.

"You look absolutely breathtaking." Wade's mom, in a pretty pale pink gown, had tears in her eyes.

"Mrs. Johnson, you're crying already, are you?"
~~~~~

Her soon to be mother-in-law pulled a tissue from her clutch purse and wiped her eyes carefully to avoid messing up her makeup. "I'm just very happy. Thank you for letting me join you for the preparations. I hope later today you can start calling me mom, or even Karen."

She couldn't call anyone else mom, but she would make an effort to call Mrs. Johnson by her first name.

Before she could tell her that, her mother stepped up in her electric blue gown with the Grecian lines that showed off her cleavage and bare arms. Lacey had touched up her roots and straightened out her hair, and Adriana had been kind enough to do her make-up. Even her eyebrows were straight. "Well, I'll be bawling like a baby as soon as I see you come down that aisle because I know my Kennie is happy."

Her mother nailed it with that statement.

Lacey clapped her hands twice. "Okay, moms. Time to take a golf cart ride to the pavilion so you can be walked down the aisle."

As her mom and Mrs. Johnson followed Lacey out, Adriana finished securing the veil above her high bun. "You look stunning. All along I thought you were the lucky one, but I can see it's really Wade." She winked and stepped back.

Ginger walked around inspecting her gown. "Sweetie, you look lovely. I'm so honored to be here to see this day."

"I wouldn't have it any other way. You're like my older sister."

Ginger laughed. "Much, much older sister, but I'll take it."

Lacey came in through the batwing doors. "Okay, Ginger, Adriana, it's time for us to head over in the wagon."

As the two other women headed for the exit, Lacey picked up

a bouquet of snapdragons, Kendra's favorite flowers. "Here you go. It's time to get into the stage coach. Jorge brought it around."

Kendra took one last look at herself in the mirror. Her mom had been right, the dress was better without the jacket. Turning, she followed Lacey out the door.

As the wagon, driven by Crystal in a tuxedo and top hat, headed for the end of the pavilion with her three bridesmaids, Kendra picked up her gown and walked to the reproduction stage coach. When she'd won the red lacquer monstrosity in a side poker game, she hadn't a clue what she would use it for, but once she saw it, she just couldn't sell it. It seemed fitting that she'd be brought to her wedding and back to her house afterwards in it.

Daisy and Sage actually looked proud to be decked out in fresh daisies and white ribbons and bows. A white harness held the team of two in place. Jorge sat on top in his own tux and top hat ready to drive. Buddy, in his rented tuxedo with yellow boutonniere, waited for her, holding the door open.

"You ready for this, kid?"

She smiled. "You bet."

Holding out his arm, he helped her ascend the three steps. She was thankful she hadn't bought a gown with a train. Once inside, Buddy folded up the steps, then hopped in and sat next to her.

As Jorge started the team forward, the memory of her and Wade making love in the coach flashed through her mind, making her suddenly feel warm.

"Who knew all those years ago when we first let you into our trailer and taught you poker that we would be here today on Poker Flat, your own nudist resort, funded by your poker winnings?" He shook his head in disbelief.

She winked. "I even won this coach in a poker game in Tombstone."

"That seems fitting somehow." Buddy chuckled.

She looked out the windows as the coach crossed the fork in the road. She'd made all this happen and fell in love, too. Despite her beginnings, and Fred, and Eugene. She'd created this place and now she'd truly share it with a man she'd never even dreamed existed. As they reached the parking area in front of the main building, the coach stopped to allow the wagon to pull up and park. There wasn't enough room between the pool area and casita path for two such large conveyances.

When they started to move again and she could see everyone sitting in the rows beneath the pavilion, her heartbeat picked up its pace. It was finally happening. The coach pulled to a stop at the end of the pavilion. Lacey cracked the door open. "Now you stay in here until Ginger starts her walk down, okay?"

She nodded her mouth suddenly dry.

Buddy took her hand and squeezed. "We've got it."

Lacey smiled. "Good luck."

"Take deep breaths, kid. It's just family and friends, the same people you had dinner with last night. The people who love you, especially that guy up there." He pointed to the end of what looked like a five-mile long aisle and her eyes found Wade.

Her breath stopped altogether as she gazed at him. He was dressed in a black tuxedo and black cowboy hat. In his left lapel was a white boutonniere, but it was his smile that had taken her breath. He was grinning from ear to ear.

As her own lips smiled back, she started to breathe again. Buddy was right, it was the very same people who'd been at dinner last night. The only new people were Cole, Lacey's husband, and the Justice of the Peace, who wore a white cowboy hat. Kendra didn't remember the older man wearing one when she'd met him. Lacey must have had a hand in that accessory.

The knot in her stomach was almost gone. She needed to marry her cowboy, and she wanted to do it now. She reached for the handle on the coach door and Buddy stopped her. "Hey, hey, not yet. You heard Lacey."

Right. Lacey. She'd already forgot her instructions and she'd put so much time and effort into the wedding.

Not able to leave, Kendra watched from her seat high above those below. Little Tierney spread yellow rose pedals down the aisle before running to her mommy and getting comfortable on her lap.

Kendra chuckled as Raine, Wade's younger sister held the leashes on Scruffy and Freckles, the latter proudly bearing a pillow with their wedding rings. "Way to go, mom." As Raine brought the dogs up to Dale, who removed the little pillow, her mom looked back to someone behind her and pointed. She was obviously very proud. Then Raine walked the dogs out of the pavilion and tied them to a post in the shade of the outdoor bar.

Next came Lacey, who set the proper pace. Adriana followed. As Ginger stepped into the aisle, Kendra looked at Buddy. "Now can we go?"

He laughed. "Yes, let me go first so I can pull the steps down for you."

She rolled her eyes. She'd been about to exit without the steps and probably would have fallen on her face.

Buddy opened the door and helped her down then shut it

behind them. Just as she linked her arm in his, the electric pianist from the band, who was set up to the side of the officiate, began to play the Wedding March.

Everyone rose and looked back at her. She swallowed hard, seeking Wade's calming gaze, but she couldn't see him.

She did see her staff though. Mac was actually in a dress and Kendra widened her eyes at her. She noticed Jorge and Selma standing next to each other, which was a huge improvement. Cole sat near the front, his eyes still glued on his wife. She also noticed Tanner and his girlfriend held hands.

As they walked, Buddy leaned in. "You're the daughter I never had. I have to tell you this is the proudest moment of my life."

She swung her gaze to his, swallowing the lump in her throat at his whispered words. "Thank you for being the dad I always wanted."

He beamed, his eyes misty. In the next moment, he was handing her over to Wade, whose gaze made her insides melt.

As he turned them to face the Justice, he lowered his head. "I told you long ago, cowboys never fold. I will hold to that until my dying breath."

Her heart swelled with joy as he straightened to take their vows.

Chapter Eleven

Thursday continued.

"I believe they're playing our song." Wade pulled her to her feet behind the head table and escorted her out to the dance floor as the lead singer announced it would be the first dance.

She smiled up at him. "Do you think you remember how to waltz?"

"That's never been my problem." He looked down at her chest covered in the white applique of the wedding gown. "I think my concentration will be a bit better."

She laughed as he moved her in time with the waltz. As he twirled her around the floor, people started clapping. She laughed as he proved to her it really had been her own body that tripped him up. When they finished the dance, he hadn't stepped on her feet once. It was perfect.

She lost her smile at the thought.

"What's wrong, Mrs. Johnson?"

It took her a second to realize Wade spoke to her. It was a great distraction. "That's right. I'm now Kendra Johnson."

"Yes, you are, and I have a little something for you. Buddy, can you grab that chair?"

Wade took the chair and placed it in front of the head table so her back was to her mom and his parents.

"Gentlemen."

She stared as Luke, Tanner, Dale, Chris, and Hunter lined up in front of her, all wearing cowboy hats. Wade was in front with Dale and Tanner.

Suddenly, the band began to play Boot Scootin' Boogie and the six men started to dance. At first, she was surprised, then nervous that Wade would mess up. But as they continued, she was shocked to see that Wade was one of the best dancers. When the men finished, everyone stood to applaud. She jumped up and gave him a hug. "You were holding out on me."

He shook his head. "No, I just don't like the waltz."

She grinned. "I'll keep that in mind."

Dale started to pull Wade away. "You guys can cuddle and all that stuff later. This man needs to talk to his grandmother before she comes out here and pulls him off the floor by the ear."

As the two men moved to a table at the edge of the dance floor, she pushed the chair back and started around the table to talk to her mom.

"Ack! Who are you?"

At Natasha's yell, she turned to find Fred staggering into the dining room, the ever-present bottle in his hand. Again? Now the man was more like a housefly than a wasp —a nuisance.

"I've come to dance with my fucking daughter." He laughed.

"That's perfect since she must be fucking that cowboy to get him to marry her."

Her gaze flew to Wade, whose face had turned as hard as the river rock in the Great Room fireplace. She wanted to tell him to ignore it, but stopped. Whatever Fred had coming to him, he deserved.

As Fred stumbled toward the front table, Wade spun him around to face him and punched him in the face. Fred's head snapped to the side as he stumbled back, losing his balance and falling backward toward the wedding cake.

She watched in surprise as his head hit the table and the cake teetered before heading for the floor.

Mac came out of nowhere, lunging forward, and picked the top tier of the five-tiered cake out of mid-air before sliding to a stop on the floor, her purple dress covered in cake.

Everyone froze, turning their gazes on her.

Irritation that Fred could ruin her perfect wedding burned through her, followed by a huge relief as the knot in her stomach disintegrated completely. *Thank you, Fred.*

She smiled as she made eye contact with everyone before shrugging at Wade. "I never said our life together would be perfect."

His lips split into a wide grin. "Nope, you didn't."

Hunter stepped forward and pulled the drunken Fred to a standing position. "I'll take him out of here."

"I'll do that." At the sound of the strange voice, they all turned to find Kane, his eyes no longer swollen, dressed in a brown cowboy hat, sleeveless tee-shirt, blue jeans and boots.

"You came." Chris' excited voice made it clear who had invited him.

"Well, hello handsome." At Adriana's comment, Hunter scowled.

She raised her hands. "I'm just making an observation."

Kane gave a small roll of his shoulders as if he was uncomfortable. "I'll take him to the airport and make sure he gets on the plane."

Obviously, Chris had filled Kane in on who Fred was.

Hunter looked to her for direction.

Kendra nodded at him. "Go ahead. It's either that or jail and I'd rather he not be so close."

Hunter walked Fred over to Kane and handed him off. "Thanks."

"I'm happy to help. Enjoy the reception." With a slight tip of his hat to everyone, he dragged Fred away.

Wade nodded to the band and they started up again as Selma, Natasha, and Crystal started to clean up the cake from the floor. Wade strode over to her. "I'm sorry I ruined our cake."

She shook her head and smiled. "Don't be sorry. It's a good omen. The wedding was going far too perfectly. Call it superstitious, but now I'm fully confident that we will last forever."

He looked at her quizzically. "If I'd known that was all it took, I would have stepped on your dress while we danced and ripped it."

She laughed. "If you think that would pull this off, you have another thing coming."

He wiggled his brows. "I'm looking forward to that."

They weren't able to pursue the subject as Lacey brought the top tier of the cake to the head table and had them feed each other cake. Seriously, the woman wasn't going to miss a beat.

Then just as Kendra thought they could relax while everyone socialized, Lacey clapped her hands. "Okay everyone. Time to say goodbye to the happy newlyweds."

She tugged on Lacey's arm and whispered. "What are you talking about? We don't have to rush off. It's not like we have far to go."

Lacey laughed. "Actually, you do." She motioned over the staff of Poker Flat. They made a semi-circle in front of her and Wade. She looked at him in question, but he just shrugged.

Lacey cleared her throat. "On behalf of all the staff you see here, we bought you two nights at the Vista del Sol Resorts and Spa Cave Creek Luxury Suites. And since it was a pretty penny, you need to go now to make the most of it."

Her throat closed, keeping her from saying a word.

Wade spoke for them, but even his voice was gruff. "Thank you. All of you."

Chris shrugged. "It was the least we could do for the people who gave us another chance."

At the nods from the whole staff, Kendra sniffed. Swallowing hard, she forced herself to speak. "Poker Flat wouldn't be what it is without you all."

Each staff member came up to wish them well. Then it was goodbyes to family and friends. Before she knew it, they were bustled off into the stagecoach and on their way.

After unlocking the door to the suite, Wade scooped Kendra up.

She grabbed him around the neck. "What are you doing?"

"I'm carrying you over the threshold. Lacey would kill me if I didn't."

She relaxed against him as he kicked the door open and strode inside. "Wow."

Her reaction echoed his own. The entire place was obviously first class. To the right, in front of sliding glass doors, was a round table with a gold champagne fountain gurgling, the chandelier over it making it sparkle. To the left was a state-of-the-art kitchen boasting a large marble island with a crystal bowl of fresh strawberries in the middle. Directly across from where they stood was a wide living room with large black leather couch and chair, cowhide coffee table, glass side tables and recessed lighting. To the left of that were double doors thrown open to reveal a king size bed. The gray blanket was pulled back to expose black satin sheets sprinkled with white rose pedals.

Wade lowered Kendra to her feet. "We will definitely have to thank our staff."

"I can't believe they did this." Her words were barely above a whisper.

He chuckled. "They were so smart to make it a surprise, otherwise you would have never left the resort."

She looked at him. "You're right. I have a hard time letting go of control."

"I can help you with that." He wiggled his brows, already eyeing the marble island.

"Uh-uh. This time, I'm in control." She took his hand and led him to the black leather couch. "I like this room. It's more masculine, which makes me feel more womanly."

Her hand on his chest pushed him and he took the hint, sitting on the couch, his cock already responding in his tuxedo pants. "You look pretty womanly to me."

She smiled seductively. "Thank you." She turned and sauntered out of the room, only to come back carrying an ice bucket with champagne bottle.

"Where'd you find that?"

"In the bedroom. I think they expect us to live on champagne and strawberries." She set it down on the end table next to him.

"I'm hoping they at least left us whip cream in the fridge."

She laughed, more relaxed than he'd seen her in a long time. "We'll have to check that out later. I'm more in the mood for you." As she licked her lips, his cock hardened.

She stepped back and kicked off her high heels. "So glad to be out of those. I think I've become addicted to cowboy boots."

Her gaze ran from his face down over his body to his black cowboy boots. "I'll help you off with yours in a minute."

"Can I help you with anything?"

She shook her head. "No, you just stay there."

As she reached her hands behind her back, he heard the sound of a zipper. He stared at the front of her dress, his erection harder now as he anticipated her reveal.

His cock jumped as the top of her dress fell forward to reveal her bare breasts. As the whole dress split in the back and crumpled to the floor, his breath caught. Kendra stood there in her veil, a lacey garter belt and white opaque hose.

Stepping from the dress, she picked it up then turned her back to him to drape it over the black leather chair. Her ass showed off the white straps of lace on the garter running down each cheek, which made his balls tighten.

She turned to face him, all bare with wisps of white.

He resisted the urge to undress and waited to see what she would do next, the anticipation feeding his growing need.

"Now, let's see about those boots." She stepped over his legs and turned her back on him, bending over to grasp the heel of his right boot.

He gazed at the soft flesh between her thighs, swearing there was moisture there. It didn't occur to him to touch her until the first boot was off. As he reached forward to stroke her smooth ass, she looked over her shoulder. "Keep your hands to yourself."

Dropping his hands, he allowed her the control she liked. He was one lucky man to have his naked bride taking care of him. He certainly wasn't going to interrupt if she didn't want him to.

Kendra pulled off his other boot then set both next to her dress. If he didn't know better, he'd swear she was bending over on purpose to entice him. And it was working.

She came back to him and spread his knees apart, then dropped down to her knees, her veil floating past his pants. Running her hands along his clothed legs, her fingers found his zipper. In short order, she had it lowered and his hard cock was bared. "Now this is what I'm hungry for."

Thinking to touch her cheek, he lifted his hand.

"I said, no hands."

At her command, he returned his hand to the couch beside him. If she wanted control, he'd let her have it…this time.

With one finger, she traced the ridge of his head before stroking downward. The sensation left him wanting so much more. She surprised him when she lowered her head, but didn't touch his cock with her mouth. Instead, she took her veil and wrapped it around him.

The light material slid along him like the inside of her sheath. He sucked in his breath as she proceeded to run it up and down the length of him. His tip leaked out his pleasure and she stopped to lick it off before continuing his exquisite torture.

"You keep that up I'm going to come without you."

She smirked. "Good, you deserve it."

Her words didn't help his control. Neither did it help when she dipped her head and licked his balls.

He tipped his head back, knocking his hat off as he tried to hold on, but it was too much. He'd be damned if he'd let go without her on their wedding night. To hell with the no hands rule.

Pulling her up by her shoulders, he pushed her onto the couch.

She grinned. "Did you want something?"

He slid his cock into her wet sheath as he came down over her, pressing her into the leather. "Yes. I want you."

Her stocking clad legs wrapped around him as she urged him to take her to his hilt. Crushing her breasts between them, he touched her lips with his own and she opened for him.

She had him so hard, he could barely control his thrusts, but he didn't need to. His wife reached her climax just a second before he did. He lifted his lips from hers to suck in the air he needed as his release rocked him, his brain registering only two things—his ecstasy and the fact she was his.

Kendra stretched beneath her cowboy, loving the feel of the leather beneath her, his hard body completely clothed over her and his cock inside her. She squeezed her sheath and his head snapped up.

"Hey, give a man a minute."

She laughed, her sheath squeezing him more, eliciting a groan. "We only have this place for a couple nights. I want to make the most of it."

"We will. I promise."

She ran her hand through his short hair. "Did I tell you how handsome you looked today?"

He appeared to think about it. "No, I can't say that you have."

"Well, you were exceptionally handsome today. I kept thinking if these women had any idea what was beneath these clothes, I'd have to fight them off."

He raised his eyebrows in disbelief. "Oh, really."

She gave him an innocent smile. "That and the fact I couldn't wait to have my husband inside me."

At her words, his warm brown gaze softened. "You made me the happiest man in the world today by becoming my wife."

It was as if her heart would burst with all the goodness she had from this man. "I wish I could have done so sooner, but I think I needed the time we had. I also needed to learn to trust my staff. Speaking of staff, did you notice who was sitting next to each other at the wedding?"

"You mean Jorge and Selma?"

"I think something might happen there. I told you she liked him."

"You were right."

She grinned. "I'm so glad to hear you say that because that means I won our bet."

His eyes widened. "That's right. You get to choose the place for our honeymoon."

Now that it was time to confess where she wanted to go, she hoped he didn't mind. "I want to go to Alaska. Not just down south, but way up north where it's cold. I want to go when it's been triple digits here for months and getting old."

"That's an excellent idea!"

"Really?" She'd been afraid he'd think it was silly. "Even if we go for a whole month?"

His brow furrowed. "Let me get this straight. You want me to leave the sweltering heat of Phoenix to go up to Alaska and spend four weeks with you?"

She nodded. When he put it like that, it didn't sound so crazy. "Yes."

"I can definitely do that, but can you?"

"I can…now."

"Now?"

She wanted him to understand. "Like I said, I trust my staff now, but I also trust myself. I've spent my life reacting to my past, basing my decisions on old pain."

He looked deeply into her eyes. "And now?"

She searched her memories for leftover hurt, but found none. "I've made peace with myself and my past. I want to concentrate on the future."

His smiled returned. "So do I, but only with you beside me."

She touched his lips with the faintest of kisses. "I'm all-in."

"I've waited a long time for you to say that to me."

Her heart hitched that she truly hadn't been able to freely give herself. "I know. I'm sorry I made you wait, but I mean it. You're stuck with me now, cowboy."

"Whatever you say, Mrs. Johnson."

She grinned at the memory of her telling him not to call her Missus when he first arrived at Poker Flat. "I really like the sound of that."

"Me, too." His stomach growled and his eyes widened. "I don't like the sound of that though."

"You didn't eat much either, did you?" She'd been so busy talking to people and doing what Lacey told her to do, that she'd barely had a bite.

"No, but I'm hoping there's a fridge full of food in there."

She sighed. "That means we're going to have to get up."

"We could always try getting over there together."

She laughed. "Get off me. I'm hungry." She pretended to try to get him off, but really all she needed was him.

Her stomach growled, too. Or maybe she needed him *and* food.

"Yes, ma'am."

As Wade left her, she didn't feel disappointed because she not only had him for two days straight, but for the rest of her life.

He held out his hand and helped her rise off the couch. "I'll pop that champagne, if you see what's in the fridge."

"That's a deal." She walked into the kitchen and opened the refrigerator to find another surprise. Her eyes grew misty again. Shit, was this what happened to a woman when she got married? Taking out the boxes, she placed them on the marble island, then started to pull out plates.

Wade, all zipped up now, strode into the kitchen with two glasses of champagne. "What's this?"

She handed him the note and he read it out loud.

"The bridal couple never have a chance to eat, but we didn't want you to miss any part of your wedding, so we packed this up for you. Lacey and Natasha." He shook his head as he stared at the card.

She put her arm around his waist and snuggled in close. "You okay?"

He nodded. When he spoke, his voice was gravely. "Just thinking about all the people and all the experiences I would have never had if I hadn't met you."

She squeezed him. "Crazy experiences that most people never have to deal with. I brought you all my baggage."

He pulled out a stool and guided her to it. "I had a bit of my own, as well."

She froze. "What? You never told me about anything besides your injuries from the rodeo."

"I know. You have had so much to handle, I didn't want to add to your worry."

Disbelief rifled through her. "I would have loved to have known I wasn't the only one with a messed-up background."

"It's not a big deal, but it's why Dale was my best man today."

Okay, maybe this was bigger than he was letting on. "I did wonder why you didn't make Luke or Tanner your best man."

Wade opened the boxes of food and started piling it on the plates. "If it wasn't for Dale, I would have never met you."

She watched his face as he concentrated on arranging the quesadillas on the plates. "I always thought you were too perfect to be a client, but when you told me you were friends, and you were doing him a favor, I understood why he sent you."

Wade nodded as he put one plate into the microwave. "I would have never worked at a nudist resort, but the favor I owed him I'm still not sure is repaid."

Now he had her worried. "Did he have to bail you out of jail?"

He chuckled, relaxing his face. "No, nothing like that. But I definitely wouldn't be married to you right now."

"You mean because you wouldn't have met me."

"No, because I would have already been married."

She stared at him in shock. "You never told me that."

"It's not something I'm proud of. I had been seeing a young woman and she got pregnant. After she had the baby, she found me and claimed it was mine. It never even occurred to me that she could be lying."

"Was she?"

"Yes, but I didn't know that. Dale refused to come to the wedding unless I had a paternity test done. He was going to be in my wedding party, so I did it. If he hadn't made that stipulation, I would have married her."

She scowled. "That's so wrong of her to use her baby to trap you."

"I know, but like I said, it never occurred to me. So once again he was very important in my wedding, which is why he was my best man."

Not only was she relieved he'd avoided marrying the wrong woman for the wrong reasons, but she was also pleased to know he wasn't quite as perfect as he seemed. Their partnership felt more real this way.

He pulled out one plate and put another in and hit the timer.

"Is there anything else I should know that you haven't told me?" They'd been together over a year and he hadn't told her that. She had to check.

He shook his head before a devilish gleam entered his eyes.

"There was this one time when these two women invited me back to their place."

Just by the look in his eye she knew he was lying. "Oh, really? And what happened."

The surprised look on his face said it all.

She laughed. "Wade, you suck at bluffing."

He came around the counter and wrapped his arms around her from behind. "I should know better than to play poker with a professional."

"Not anymore. Now I'm just that Mrs. Johnson who owns a nudist resort."

"And what a looker she is, too."

She looked over her shoulder at him. "Even without clothes on?"

His hands moved up to cup her breasts. "That's how she looks the best."

As his fingers found her nipples, his mouth descended on her neck, and soon he was using the marble island just like he wanted, their dinner forgotten, and she couldn't have cared less.

EPILOGUE

Wade drove down the dirt road off the Carefree Highway toward Poker Flat. Their short honeymoon changed Kendra. Or maybe it was the wedding, or both. Now he felt a lot more confident in his gift to her.

Halfway down the dirt road, he turned off onto a pseudo-path into the desert.

Kendra grabbed the handle above her door to hold on as he drove over bumps. "Wade, where are you going?"

"I want to show you something."

She bounced in the seat as they hit another bump. "You do know we're trespassing, right?"

He didn't answer, instead focusing on the barely-there path toward a stand of juniper trees. When he reached them, he stopped the truck.

"I'm not sure this is a good idea." He still had a tight grip on the handle. "The man who owns this property is a curmudgeon."

He chuckled silently as he opened his door. "And how do you know that?"

"Because I tried to buy this land from him. I thought these trees would hide the resort." She finally released the handle and unbuckled her seatbelt. "That was before I found the land in the ravine, so it turned out for the best. Now the old man has a nudist resort as a neighbor. Karma's a bitch." She smirked, blatantly pleased with Karma.

He jumped out and walked around to open her door. "So you liked this spot?" His heart beat faster, his excitement building after learning that tidbit of information.

She stepped out and adjusted her brown cowboy hat. Quickly, she scanned the area, obviously a little concerned. "Yes, I do like it, though now I see the juniper grove would have been too small to hide all of Poker Flat. Still, it's a nice spot. Why? The man I talked to would probably shoot first and ask questions later, so if you want to show me something, we better do it fast."

He took her hand and led her to stand in front of the grove. "This is it."

She looked at the trees then looked at him. "This is what? A grove of trees. I know."

He shook his head, finally allowing himself to grin. "This is the spot for our new house."

She blinked, then opened her mouth then closed it. She looked at the trees and back at him.

He laughed, unable to contain it. "I bought this property with some of the money I saved for a ranch."

"Wade." Her voice was barely above a whisper. "I thought you *wanted* a ranch."

He took her in his arms, letting his hands rest on her lower back. "I did want a ranch because that was what every cowboy wants one day, but what you created is so much more unique and challenging."

"You mean all encompassing."

He nodded. "That too, which is why I bought this property. We can build a house here and actually be away from work, yet still be close enough in an emergency."

She rolled her eyes. "You mean like when the sheriffs have to come to take away trespassers or Detective Anderson has to investigate suspected criminal activity?"

Lucky, the good detective hadn't had to visit in almost a year. "Yes. Also, with so much acreage, we could build your mom a small place, too."

Kendra looked away.

Now that wasn't the reaction he had hoped for. "What is it?"

When she looked back at him there were tears in her eyes. "You're so much better than I ever dreamed a husband could be."

He pulled her tight. "And you're so much more than I expected to have in a wife." He pulled back. "Does that mean you like the idea?"

"Oh, I love this. It's just what I wanted. Maybe we could even work more similar hours and have a real life outside of the resort." Her voice rose with her excitement.

He lowered his lips to within inches of hers. "That sounds perfect."

She chuckled before he closed the deal with a kiss. She tasted like the coffee she had with breakfast as her tongue met his. His nostrils filled with the almond-rose scent of her, reminding him of the bath she'd given him.

He finally pulled away. As much as he wanted to make love to her on their property, he'd prefer they had at least something started on their home, even if it was just a camp. "I believe you were anxious to get back to work?"

She opened her eyes and frowned. "Me? That was you."

He waited, knowing she wouldn't be able to keep up the pretense.

Her lips quirked. "Okay, it was me. We should get back. Guests came in this morning and we need to see how everyone is doing."

He let go and took her hand to walk back to his truck. "I'm thinking we should probably give Lacey a vacation. Getting paid a big bonus for planning a wedding is a good start, but I have a feeling she wouldn't mind a few extra days." He opened the passenger door.

"Yes, and I want to see if Dale has sent me any resumes yet. We need to hire more staff."

He closed her door then jumped in the driver's seat. He looked at his wife. His *wife*. "I think we need to make another agreement."

She cocked her head. "We do? What kind of agreement?"

"We both work hard, but if we want this land to be truly ours and not an extension of Poker Flat, I suggest that whenever we come on this land, we no longer discuss the resort. What do you think?" He held his breath, knowing exactly what kind of workaholic his wife was.

"I agree, with the exception of those emergencies."

He leaned over and gave her a quick kiss. "You are one special woman."

She smirked at him. "I know."

Laughing, he turned the key and headed to Poker Flat.

~~~~~

Kendra shuffled through the invoices Lacey left in her in-box. Nothing unexpected was in there, but then again, they'd only been gone one business day. It looked like everything was well in order. With no fires to put out, she turned to something more important, Wade's wedding gift.

Rising, she walked over to the locked filing cabinet in the corner of her office. She opened the third drawer down and pulled it all the way out. Finding the file she wanted, she opened it and put the contents on Wade's desk.

"I saw Wade, so that means Kennie is back. Did you see where she went?"

At her mom's voice carried down the hall and into the open door of her office. She closed the drawer, ready to greet her mom.

"Well, shit."

At her mom's words, she took a step toward her door when Scruffy and Freckles ran inside.

Her heart skidded to a halt. Her automatic response finally overtaken by the memory of the coyote she'd chased away. She didn't have to be afraid anymore. As she stood there, the dogs ran to her and jumped up, their tongues hanging out.

Hesitantly, she put her hand down to pet one of them, only to have it licked. Smiling, she crouched down and they pushed her over with their exuberance.

"Well, I'll be a jackpot run wild. Will you look at that."
~~~~~

She looked up from the floor to find her mother staring at her with a wide grin on her face. "I'm not afraid anymore."

"So I see. Why?"

She shrugged. "I had another run in with a coyote." She scratched Scruffy's head before looking up again. "I won this time."

Her mother beamed. "Well, you're a lot bigger now. I'm glad you're back. Believe it or not, I missed you."

She rose from the floor and gave her mom a hug. "I won't be leaving again anytime soon."

"Good because we have a lot to talk about, including why you didn't tell me that your asshole father had shown up twice before the wedding and how come Jorge is giving me the cold shoulder, and who is this Kane person exactly?"

Kendra guided her mom out of the office, the dogs following her. "Why don't I bring dinner over and my husband and I will fill you in on everything."

Her mom stopped and covered her eyes. "I don't want to hear about your honeymoon."

She stifled a chuckle. The last she knew, her mom didn't listen with her eyes. "You can take your hands away mom, I wasn't going to tell you about our wedding night. We're actually taking a honeymoon in August. Even then, I'll only tell you about the highlights."

Her mom dropped her hands. "Well good. I know you have to unpack and get to work, so I'm going out to the bar to get me some more sex ed. Your Adriana is one smart lady."

She watched her mom cross into the Great Room with the dogs before turning toward the reception desk to find Lacey and Wade staring at her. "What?"

Lacey pointed after her mother. "You had the dogs running around your feet."

"Yes, I did." She winked at Wade. "I learned a little something from a coyote."

He smiled. "Ah, that makes sense."

Lacey looked at them both as if they'd lost it.

Kendra laughed. "Come here, cowboy, I have something for you to see."

Wade followed her down to their office. "If it's a repair order, put it aside until Monday, but if it's what you're wearing under that shirt then move faster."

"Wade, behave. We're not in the suite anymore."

"It was worth a shot."

She stopped next to his desk. "Take a look." Now that the moment had come, she was nervous. Had she done the right thing?

He moved behind it and looked at the pile of papers. Sitting, he picked them up and read. After a few minutes, he stopped. "Is this true? I'm now an equal owner of Poker Flat Nudist Resort?"

At his serious expression, her chest tightened. She nodded. "I hope you're okay with that."

He took her hand in his. "I'm thrilled and humbled that you'd share all of this with me."

"I want us to be equal partners in everything. You're my husband and that's how it should be. I'm hoping we can do this marriage thing right."

A devilish gleam appeared in his eyes. "Equal partners in *everything*?"

Oh, no. "What are you thinking?"

He pulled her around to his side of the desk, spreading his

knees to capture her legs. "I'm thinking that we should celebrate. First we make love on my desk and then we make love on yours."

Her heart swelled. "I like the way you think."

Sweeping the papers into his top drawer, Wade sat her on the desk and proceeded to undress her until she simply couldn't think at all.

Read on for Kendra and Wade's love story and the opening of Poker Flat in Cowboys Never Fold.

CHAPTER ONE

Wade Johnson slowed his Chevy Silverado and stared at the wooden sign with burnt-in letters hanging above the dirt road: POKER FLAT NUDIST RESORT.

It swung between two weathered posts, the sign's newness jolting the senses against the Old West background.

Stopping his pickup, he hesitated to make the left turn. His best friend had called in a big favor. Nine years ago, Wade had been blinded by love and almost made the worst mistake of his life. If it hadn't been for Dale's instincts and a paternity test, Wade would have been shackled to a selfish sorority girl and left with another man's kid. Shit, he could have been a country song.

He owed Dale and he'd never back out on a friend, even if it meant working at a nudist resort for three months. "I *am* doing this." The sound of his voice gave him the boost he needed. With his commitment firmly in place despite a dozen misgivings, he turned the truck down the dirt road.

At least the pay was outstanding, and he could choose his own horseflesh and set up the stables as he felt they should be run. Just the thought of starting a new operation had him stepping on the gas a bit harder, his truck throwing up a cloud of dust that could probably be seen in Wickenburg.

After a good mile of nothing but desert, a wooden barrier declared the end of the road. To the right was an overly large garage with only three sides. He brought the truck to a stop underneath the shelter. It could clearly house a couple dozen cars and the massive metal structure was tall enough for RVs too. The roof had to be at least twenty feet high.

Exiting his vehicle, his boots hit concrete. Nice. If this is how the owner built the garage, he couldn't wait to see the new stables. Dale's voice in his head dampened his enthusiasm. *I've sent three men out there to set up this woman's stables and all three quit. This could kill my temp agency's reputation. I need someone I can trust to find out what's going on. If she is a cranky old bitch who expects miracles, I don't need her as a client. But if it's something else, I want to know. If her resort takes off, I plan to be the one filling her staffing needs.*

Wade straightened his black Stetson and walked toward the old man sleeping on a chair in the relative coolness of the structure. It was August and days in the desert usually hit three digit degrees. The sound of his boots hitting the floor didn't wake the man, so he shook him.

"What? What? I don't knows nothin.'" The man's eyes were a bit glazed and his chin showed a few days of beard growth.

Wade tipped his hat. "Afternoon. I'm Wade Johnson. Dale Osborn sent me to set up the stables here."

The man stood and teetered before steadying himself with the folding chair. "I'm Billy." The smell of alcohol was faint but definitely there. Billy thrust out his hand as if suddenly remembering his manners.

Wade shook, taking in the faded blue jeans, ripped sneakers

and dirty t-shirt. He sincerely hoped Billy wouldn't be the one greeting the guests. "Where would I find the owner?"

The short man stared at him for a few moments. "Right. Right. Come on. I'll takes you down."

Down? Wade followed Billy to a tan golf cart and got in. As they proceeded out of the garage, he looked everywhere for the supposed resort, but there was nothing but desert for miles, and no butte stood out to hide it.

Then they drove past the wooden barricade and after a few minutes he recognized the edges of what must have been a hundred-year-old ravine that had weathered away to create a small canyon. As they drew closer to the ledge, the resort came into view.

"Wow." It was an ingenious design. One that had him rethinking a few of his own plans for a spread.

Billy smiled a toothy grin. "Yup. That be what everyone says."

Wade shook his head in astonishment. Across the ravine, near the top was a natural shelf of land where a large building, pool and stables sat surrounded by green lawn and narrow pathways for walking. Below that shelf was another that was home to small cottages sporadically placed among the natural desert landscape. There were more walking trails going farther into the small canyon. At the bottom was a creek with a strip of green growth on each side.

"How long did it take to build this place?"

Billy frowned. "If you counts the stonewallin' from the county, two years. But when the permits was in place and legit, the construction took a year. The stables is the newest building." He pointed to the white structure.

Wade's stomach tensed with excitement. A new barn, corral

and soon horses of his choosing without spending a dime of his own money was too enticing to pass up, not that he would. Dale's company was new and he needed a good reputation if he was to succeed in Phoenix. Wade owed him and he would stay long enough to discover why the other stablemen left. That Wade would enjoy the job he was hired for was a bonus. He could already see possibilities for trails down to the creek. How far did it go?

"We could has opened sooner if we has reli…help we can depend on. I hope you plan to stay longer than the last horse man." Billy spat over the side of the cart. "We needs someone we can count on out here."

He looked at Billy and his excitement dimmed. "Was the stable manager quitting the only thing that held everything up?"

"Nah. We gots a nosey sheriff and stupid stuff breaks every day." Billy slowed the cart as they drove around a switchback. After the cart rumbled across a well-made wooden bridge that spanned the creek, Billy pointed at the road. "This here path were designed for the wagon and stagecoach. Only the employees gets to drive those. The golf carts, them is for the guests."

"Stagecoach?" Wade scanned the resort as they drove closer, expecting to see the oddity sitting on the verdant lawn.

Billy broke into a big grin, revealing a missing tooth on the left side. "You betcha. Prettiest darn thing I has ever seen. It's a repro…copy of one of them Old West ones. You be in charge of it. Maybe you can give me a ride in it? Miss Kendra don't lets me drive that one."

Wade silently agreed with Miss Kendra's decision. There were a lot of the woman's decisions he agreed with, so why did she have such a hard time keeping staff when she hadn't even opened? It couldn't be because of the nude clientele. She didn't have any yet. He would never have taken a job at a nudist resort if Dale hadn't needed him. People walking around nude in public wasn't his thing.

Oh shit. What if the resort was the owner's retirement dream come true and she ran the place nude? Now that was a sight he wasn't in a hurry to see.

"Here you be. Miss Kendra through that there pavilion. At least, that where I sees her last. She were bossing over the buildin' of some water thingy by the pool. Whatever it are, I sure when she be done, it will look good."

Wade stepped out and tipped his hat. "Thank you." As Billy drove away, Wade shook his head. How could the old man obviously idolize the owner and yet others quit on her? He strolled in the direction Billy indicated. He appreciated the view the resort presented, but he mentally braced himself for encountering a naked old woman.

As he turned the corner at the end of the freestanding pavilion, he found the pool, its crystal-clear water actually making him thirsty. The large rectangle had a curvy pool coming off it that imitated a winding river. Every eight feet or so a concrete high-table broke the surface of the water. Talk about an enticement to drink. Whatever kind of personality this woman had, he would be the first to admit she was smart.

He approached a group of three men with Desert Pool Design emblazoned on their shirts. They rested in the shade, chowing down on sandwiches. "Good afternoon. Could you tell me where to find Miss Kendra Lowe?"

One of the men pointed, his mouth full.

"Thanks."

Wade strode toward the bar. It was under another pavilion, but this one attached to the main building and its far side was supported by stone columns. The sleek wood bar top was at least three inches of ironwood. The rattling of glasses came from behind it but he couldn't see anyone.

"Hello there. I'm looking for Miss Kendra Lowe?"

A young woman stood up from behind the bar, her disheveled dark brown hair caught in a clip behind her head. She wiped sweat from her brow with the back of a dirty hand. It seemed everything was clean but the workers. She gazed at him, no curiosity whatsoever in the deep blue of her eyes. "I'm Kendra Lowe."

Wade couldn't help staring in disbelief. Out of habit, he wiped his hand on his jeans although it was probably cleaner than hers. "Good afternoon, Ms. Lowe. I'm Wade Johnson. Your new stable manager."

She studied him as she shook his hand, her expression revealing nothing.

He, on the other hand, didn't expect the owner of such a pristine spread to be so young, maybe thirty or so, almost his age. Her mouth was wide with a straight nose above it. She had very high cheekbones, but her face held none of the lines of a woman used to manual work, which she appeared to be doing. Her arms were toned, almost muscular as revealed by the modest black tank she wore, though nothing could truly hide the substantial chest it covered. But she was too thin by half, as his grandmother would say.

She placed one dirty hand on her waist and jutted out her hip, giving it a curve that wasn't there before. "So, Cowboy, it appears Dale was successful in finding me another stable manager. Good. I don't have much time left before we open and the trails still need to be chosen, the horses need to be purchased and transported, feed needs to be ordered and a ton of other details I have no clue about. I must have someone who is going to stay at least three months. Can you commit to that, no matter what?"

A surge of adrenaline shot through his body again when she mentioned picking horses. He could pretty much stay however long she needed for a chance to do that. "Yes, Ms. Lowe, I can."

"Good. I can't be worrying about that side of the operation, so you just tell me what you need, Cowboy, and we'll make it happen." She turned toward the main building. "Lacey!"

Wade stared at his new boss. This was a dream job to any cowboy worthy of riding, which made it harder to understand why so many before him quit. Maybe she was really a micromanager and pretended not to be. Or maybe she was too hard to read. Her eyes, a nice royal blue, were anything but windows to her soul. There was no smile of welcome or satisfaction. Even her tone of voice didn't give away anything.

A petite blonde woman came through the glass door of the building and smiled warmly as she approached. "Howdy, I'm Lacey."

Now that was the kind of greeting he liked. He shook her hand, careful not to squeeze too hard.

Kendra leaned on the bar, her substantial chest supported by the dark wood. "Lacey will show you your living quarters. Then become familiar with the stables, corrals and your office. We can meet around nine tonight to discuss next steps."

"Nine, yes Ms. Lowe." He nodded, not sure what to make of the late hour, but she was the boss.

Lacey hooked her arm in his. "Right this way."

"And Cowboy." They'd only taken a couple steps, when Kendra stopped them. "Don't call me Ms. Lowe. It makes me sound like a teacher or something. Kendra will do."

He tipped his hat. "I can do that if you can call me Wade."

Kendra's face didn't even twitch. He waited for a sign from her that she understood. Finally, she nodded once. "Fair enough. See you at nine, Wade."

Kendra watched Wade leave, his tight butt impossible to ignore. Once he was through the glass door into the main building, she let herself slither back over the edge of the bar to sit on the floor. Damn, the man was hot. Why had Dale stopped sending her old codgers? The last thing she needed now was a distraction.

And Wade Johnson was definitely a distraction. His clean-shaven chin could serve as artwork. His brown eyes, which matched his short hair, reminded her of milk chocolate and his voice had her muscles wanting to melt. Thank God she'd been behind the bar because what really had her libido revving was his broad shoulders. Only a muscular man could be that thin at the waist and have such broad shoulders. Dammit. She hadn't had sex since she bought Poker Flat and she'd be damned if she'd have it now with some hunky cowboy employee. The odds were stacked against that working out well.

Refocusing, she pulled the small cooler back into place, assuring it would drain through the floor and not all over it. At least she wouldn't have to worry about the cowboy being underfoot. He had his domain and she had hers. She just needed to make it through their meeting tonight. After wiping her hands on her work jeans, she picked up the glass washer and set it in the sink. The plumber would be in tomorrow morning to take care of installing the final pieces of the bar according to code. Luckily, she had the liquor license from the last owner of the Poker Flat Bar, which had been located where her garage now stood. That license was worth every penny she'd paid for the ramshackle building she tore down.

And having Adriana as the bartender of her new bar should keep the liquor sales high, *if* the woman kept her clothes on. Kendra wiped her hands on a bar towel and shook her head. She had quite the crew here, but she knew all of them and their weaknesses. All she had to do is discover Wade Johnson's weakness and she could feel comfortable because right now he seemed too perfect and that would never work here. She threw the towel over the towel rack and stepped out from behind the bar.

Thankfully, she'd instituted the rule that all employees must be clothed while on shift. She'd found that tidbit in her research on nudist resorts. There was no way she'd be able to keep her hands off her new cowboy if he decided to get naked. And there was no way Adriana would be able to keep her legs closed with that man around. A former prostitute, Adriana still loved sex, but she also loved not having to do it for the money.

As if she'd known she was being thought of, Adriana pushed open the glass door to the outdoor/indoor bar. She held a tray of glasses filled with what appeared to be iced tea. Her skimpy jean shorts and red-checkered halter had her looking like a Mexican Daisy Duke. Kendra admired the woman on that level. Her comfort with her sexuality was impressive. As a teenager, Kendra's own substantial chest had simply added to her aura of trailer trash so she kept it well covered most of the time.

"Hey, boss, I thought the pool workers would like a refreshing cold drink." Adriana raised her hand. "All non-alcoholic, of course."

"Fine, but then they need to get back to work. They've been eating their lunches for an hour. I'm not paying them to take a siesta."

"You got it." Adriana's smile was wide as she tossed her straight black hair over her shoulder and sauntered out beyond the pavilion.

Kendra shook her head and sighed before heading inside. She could tell Adriana was much happier than she'd been when Kendra met her in Storey County, Nevada, during a small poker tournament. She hadn't planned on playing that one, but at the last minute had skipped Reno to avoid a possible awkward meeting with her ex-husband. When she decided to open a nudist resort, Adriana had come to mind immediately as someone who wouldn't care about a bunch of naked people running around.

Striding through the large gathering room with its twelve-foot-wide stone fireplace, Kendra allowed herself a secret smile. The contractor had thought the fireplace would be too big, but even he acknowledged how awesome it looked in the great room. It had become the centerpiece of the main building.

Walking through one of the cozy dining rooms, she pushed open the batwing doors to the kitchen. The spotless, stainless steel area was the domain of her cook, Selma, who was, as usual, muttering to herself in Spanish.

Kendra opened the refrigerator and grabbed a protein shake. She hadn't had lunch, but she didn't have time to stop for it either. Walking over to the shiny dishwasher, she listened to the hum as it sanitized its contents then crouched and looked beneath it to be sure everything was draining properly. Two nights ago, that had not been the case. If it was having issues, she would add it to her list for the plumber tomorrow. All appeared fine, so that meant one less task for the man.

She stood, then walked to where Selma cut vegetables on the stainless steel counter. She went at the food like a lumberjack at a tree, but Kendra couldn't fault the results. "Selma, any other plumbing problems I need to have the plumber take a look at tomorrow?"

The older woman didn't stop slicing. "Yeah, the hand sink is clogged. There's no fucking reason why it should be that way. I only wash my hands there. I take as good care of my kitchen here as I did of my girls in Carlin. I'm telling you, either there is a curse upon this place, or someone is messing with us."

Selma's brothel had been the best on Interstate 80 until, according to the ex-madam, a curse had been laid upon it. So it was no surprise this was her latest theory regarding the many hiccups they'd encountered in getting the resort ready, but Kendra honestly believed it was simply how things went these days. Faulty products, ignorant installers, cracks due to shipping, etcetera, had easily explained the hurdles she'd had to jump over. "Okay, I'll have him look at it tomorrow. Hopefully, that will be the end of it."

Selma grumbled something unintelligible that Kendra had a feeling wasn't meant for her ears, so she grabbed up her shake and took a swallow as she exited the kitchen. Striding toward the front desk, she noticed Wade and Lacey getting into a golf cart. Now why did Lacey have to show him where the stables were? Couldn't he see them for himself?

Irritation had her taking another swallow. Pushing open one of the tall tinted doors that welcomed visitors to the resort, she stepped out into the heat.

Lacey was explaining. "Don't worry, it's actually a rule that we keep our clothes on during our shift. Just be forewarned, Adriana does like men, so you may want to be on your guard with her."

Wade smiled. "Good to know."

Kendra gritted her teeth. The cowboy didn't need a personal escort to the stables. Her bookkeeper/receptionist had a lot of work to do. "Lacey, did you show Wade his casita?"

The pretty girl started as if she'd been caught doing something she shouldn't. "Oh, I didn't know you were here. Yes, I did. I was going to explain the stables to Wade, but I need to reconcile the bedding shipment with what we received."

Kendra's muscles relaxed. "Go ahead and do the shipment. I'll point out the way. We're shorthanded as it is and your abilities are critical to Poker Flat."

Lacey blushed. "Okay. Thanks."

As Lacey walked into the building, Kendra studied the cowboy. He considered her with equal interest, but it wasn't admiration. He appeared puzzled and that gave her a certain amount of satisfaction. She never revealed her hand.

Strolling over to the cart, she took one more swallow of her shake. "Have you ever driven a golf cart?"

The brim of his hat shaded his face, but his expression was easily read. "Yes, actually. I helped my little sister with a few of her golf tournament fundraisers."

Oh boy, this cowboy was far too good for the likes of Poker Flat. One more reason for her to stay away. "Good. Then take the path marked with the horse's head. We made all the signs easy for guests to follow."

He looked at the sign, putting his face in profile again. Shit, he was as handsome from the side as from the front. She had the unusual urge to nip at his jawline.

"That's smart. I wish all vacation spots did that."

His compliment surprised her, and she shifted her weight to her right leg, jutting out her hip. "I had to do that because our employee base isn't large and I didn't want to waste staff positions on golf cart drivers."

He turned back to her and smiled. "Another smart idea."

Completely uncomfortable with his praise and inviting smile, she ignored his comment. "In your office you should find enough to get started. Make a list of anything there you need as well as anything else for marking trails and suggestions for horses. I plan on having guests chauffeured from the garage to the resort in a wagon and I want to offer trail rides for those who are more adventurous. Remember, all guests will be nude, so if there are any special supplies we need in order to make sitting a horse comfortable, write them down too."

His smile disappeared. "Wait, you want people to ride horses while naked?"

"Of course. This is a nudist resort."

"I'm sorry, but you can't do that."

She opened her mouth to tell him she could do whatever she wanted, but he kept talking.

"If a person rides naked, they will have burns not only on their legs where they brush the saddle, but also in other areas that I guarantee you they will not be happy about."

She pondered that for a moment. Maybe that was why no other resort offered nude horseback riding, why Buddy and Ginger had longed for that experience so much. So if she could figure it out, it would make her place even more unique than it was. "I'm sure we can come up with a way around that. We'll go over it tonight."

He frowned and her stomach tensed. "Dinner is at six. Don't be late. You don't want to miss Selma's cooking and you don't want to make her mad at you either."

"Why Ms. Lowe?"

"Trust me. I was late one night and I found my quesadilla riddled with hot pepper sauce so fiery it burned my mouth for two days. You're better off not showing up at all."

He grinned and her stomach relaxed. "Okay, I'll be on time."

"Good, and Wade…"

"Yes."

"I'm not high society and I'm not married anymore, so as I said before, we can drop the Ms. Lowe."

He bowed his head and she could have sworn he was hiding a smile, but when he looked at her, he was dead serious. "I'll remember that, Kendra."

Her throat closed as he spoke her name, a strong rush of heat invading her body. Nodding once, she turned around and strode back to the building, throwing her empty shake can in the trash outside before stepping into the coolness of the resort.

Damn, she liked the sound of her name on his lips. Staying away from that cowboy was going to be very, very hard.

Read on for an excerpt from Christmas with Angel (Last Chance #1)

CHAPTER ONE

Last Chance Ranch, Arizona
December 23rd

Cole Hatcher added two pillows to the makeshift bed of sleeping bags on the hay. He'd unzipped each and spread them out so he and Lacey could crawl in together. Maybe if they could have a little privacy, they could settle their Christmas issue.

He'd pilfered all the snowflake decorations from the tree inside and hung them from the beams. In his mind, he'd envisioned it to look like it was snowing, but in reality, it looked like plastic, glass and felt snowflakes hanging from beams. Lacey would get it though. She couldn't expect more than this from her cowboy.

Adjusting the garland around the stall walls, he pulled over the small table he used for grooming the horses and placed it next to the bed. With a rag he'd grabbed from the house, he wiped it off and placed a bottle of wine on it with two plastic cups. "That should do it." His Christmas Eve present was ready, though a few hours early.

Stuffing the rag in his back pocket, he turned the battery-operated lantern to low and set it next to the wine. "Perfect."

As he headed out of the barn, the six horses in residence paid him no heed except for Angel. Her wary eyes watched him until he was out of sight.

Giving Angel to Lacey had been the best thing he'd done for that horse, besides take her from her owner. She was so fearful of men that her bond with Lacey had grown strong.

Now if he could just get his fiancé onto the same page with him, life would be great again.

Cole strode across the dirt yard, the only sound to break the crisp night air, the two note call of a whippoorwill. The quiet beckoned him, but he needed Lacey to truly enjoy it. The house lights should have been welcoming but with his two cousins in residence, one baby, Billy and his grandparents, the four bedroom house was packed.

He took the stairs to the porch two at a time. Pulling back the screen door, he opened the heavy, ironwood front door. As he stepped in, he had to stop himself from stepping back out.

The baby cried upstairs while his two cousins, Logan and Trace argued. A door slammed on the upper level then Trace stomped down the stairs, yelling back over his shoulder, "I'll be watching the game with Grandpa if you come to your senses!" He nodded to Cole as he passed by.

Old Billy, who used to work and live at Poker Flat and had just spent two months in rehab for alcoholism, ambled through the front hall from the kitchen, a bottle of water in his hand and a smile on his face. The television in the living room clicked on just as Billy entered and the volume increased substantially.

Cole winced, the noise level and activity in the house was almost painful. Like Lacey, he couldn't wait for their own home to be completed, but it barely had walls and was far too incomplete for them to have the privacy and quiet they needed. Since Lacey had given up her casita at the Poker Flat Nudist Resort, they had nowhere to go…except the barn.

She was probably in their room where she always retreated right after dinner to crunch numbers, do research, or iron clothes for work. He ran up the stairs, excited to show her the present he'd arranged, and opened the door to the bedroom.

Lacey stood next to the bed, her deep pink sweater fitting her like a second-skin, wisps of blonde hair escaping her long braid. Her maroon skirt flowed about her, accentuating her delicate femininity. He still couldn't believe this hot woman was his. She had a basket of laundry dumped out on their bed, clean clothes strewn over the quilt and a small pile folded to her right. He walked straight to her and wrapped his arms around her waist from behind. "I have a surprise for you."

She stilled then sighed. "Is it ear plugs?"

He kissed her neck beneath her ear, loving how tiny she felt against him. "Even better."

She dropped his fire department t-shirt and turned in his arms. "Better is good." She lifted her arms around his neck. "Don't get me wrong. I love your family. There just seems to be so many of them in this particular house. And now that Billy's here, it makes it very cramped."

He looked into her light brown eyes that reminded him of amaretto. "You love my family? Even my parents?"

She lowered her lashes and stared at his chest.

Damn, he needed to wait to discuss that. Talking about his parents only brought up what his mother had done to break them apart. That didn't set the mood he wanted. He wouldn't press it now. "So aren't you a little bit curious about my surprise?"

She lifted her gaze to meet his. "Is this my Christmas Eve present?"

His family had always exchanged gifts on Christmas day, but maybe he and Lacey could start their own tradition. "Yes, just a few hours early."

She looked over her shoulder at the clock sitting on the nightstand. "Only three hours and seventeen minutes early. Should I wait?"

He started to grin but it turned to a grimace as his cousin's baby let out an ear-piercing wail. "You might be able to, but I can't."

At the sound of the baby's scream, Lacey buried her head against his chest. She lifted it to look up at him. "I could use a surprise right about now."

"Good." He kissed her on the forehead then let her go so he could take her hand. As he took a step toward the door, she resisted. "I thought you were going to give me a surprise."

"We have to go outside for this."

She pointed to the pile of clothes. "But I need to finish folding the laundry."

"Leave them. This is more important."

"Okay." She let him pull her down the hall.

When they got to the top of the stairs, he released her hand and stepped aside so she could descend first. Another screeching wail sounded from above, and they both picked up their pace. As he opened the front door, the television volume increased another decimal in the living room and from the corner of his eye he caught sight of Billy who had joined his grandfather and Trace.

Lacey stepped onto the porch and sighed.

No sooner had he closed the door than she placed her hand on his chest. "Do you hear that?"

He listened. The quiet was almost deafening until four hoots, sounding like a bouncing ball, broke the silence. "You mean the Screech Owl?"

She smiled slyly. "No, I mean the quiet."

He grinned. "Wait until you see my surprise." He took her hand and they walked down the steps toward the barn.

"I hope you didn't get me another horse. I'm very attached to Angel and I think she'd get jealous."

He shook his head. "No, it's not a horse. Luckily, I haven't had any calls this week. Maybe the Christmas spirit has people being kinder to their animals." He frowned at the thought of what else the Christmas season brought. "Now if we could just get Christmas tree fires under control, everyone could have a happy Christmas."

She squeezed his hand. "I've never understood the need for a live evergreen tree in the Arizona desert. It's so dry. If a person wants to smell evergreens, they can always go up to Prescott for the day or take a hike right here in our own mountains."

"You make the house smell great with those scented candles you use. I'm glad you found them in the glass jars."

She stopped at the entrance to the barn and looked at him. "Can you turn off the firefighter tonight and give me the cowboy who loves to save abused, hurt, and unwanted horses?"

He grinned sheepishly. "I'll try. Actually, your surprise is definitely from the cowboy." He winked.

Lacey's gaze roamed over him, and he couldn't help but count himself lucky all over again. To have found her a second time, at a fire no less, had been sheer luck. That she was just as dedicated to his horse rescue ranch as he was, was a bonus. Her wizardry with the finances had also improved their solvency. But to have captured her heart once more against all odds was the greatest luck of all. "If you keep looking at me like that, your surprise might have to wait."

She widened her eyes. "Like what?" She even batted her lashes.

He laughed and pulled her into his embrace. "I love you, soon-to-be Lacey Hatcher."

"I know." She stood on tiptoe to give him a kiss.

When she didn't deepen the kiss, he had to stop himself from lowering his lips to hers again. The open barn door was not the place to start making love to his woman. Reluctantly, he released her, but grasped her hand again.

After pulling the large door closed behind him, he led Lacey through the barn, passing the filled stalls until she slowed by Angel. He understood and let go, continuing toward the last stall, not wanting to disturb the bond between her and the rescued horse.

No sooner had Lacey turned toward the white Arabian, than Angel gave a soft nicker and walked to the stall door. Lacey pet the badly marred head, cooing to her like one would talk with a baby.

Cole never tired of watching their connection. He had almost given up hope that Angel would ever interact with humans again after the abuse she'd take from her former owner. That the horse came into his life shortly after he had found Lacey again made him think it was fate. Though the horse shied away from men, she completely trusted Lacey.

When Lacey finished, she walked slowly toward him, or was she sauntering toward him? Shit, his muscles tensed in anticipation.

She still wore her clothes from work, her long skirt swishing against her white cowboy boots. The sweater showed off her figure even if it didn't reveal even a hint of cleavage. It was hard to believe she worked at a nudist resort. He was thankful once again that the resort had a strict policy about employees keeping their clothes on during work. He would go insane if Lacey was supposed to work nude. On the other hand, because Kendra owned the nudist resort she was expected to be nude. He had no idea how Wade handled his fiancé being naked half the day. Cole couldn't do it.

But Lacey was sexy even with her clothes on, especially after a long day, when her braid had loosened and her messy wheat-colored hair made it look as if she'd just spent an hour in bed with him.

He watched her eyes closely as she approached. Her gaze was riveted to him and his chest puffed with pride. When she licked her lips, he had to force himself to stay still as every tendon pushed at him to move.

Finally, her gaze flitted to the stall behind him and her lips formed a pleased smile. "Oh Cole, it's the best present you could have given me."

He released the breath he'd been holding and opened his arms. "You like it?"

She walked straight into his embrace. "I love it."

"It might get a little chilly tonight."

She shrugged. "That's why I have you to keep me warm."

"Just to keep you warm?" He frowned. "I was hoping to start a fire inside you."

Lacey's short intake of breath had his cock taking notice.

She wrapped her arms around his neck. "You are as good at starting fires as putting them out."

"Only for you." He lowered his head and kissed her.

She pressed her body against him and pushed her tongue between his lips. He caught it with his own.

Every nook of her mouth was like new territory. He tasted the tartness of the wine she had with dinner and a flavor that was all Lacey. His hands roamed over her back, feeling her sweater slide against silk.

His cock hardened at the thought of what his Racy Lacey might be wearing underneath.

She pulled her lips away abruptly. "You have too many clothes on."

"I was thinking the same about you." He wiggled his brow. "I bet I can take my shirt off faster than you can." He let his arm go slack in anticipation of the race. They were always betting about sex.

She kept her arms around him. "And what does the winner get?"

"I'm thinking, choice of position." At his words, a shiver ran through her body, sending lightning straight to his balls.

"On the count of three. One. Two. Three."

No sooner had she dropped her arms than he reached back and pulled his flannel over his head. One button pinged across the stall, hitting the wood, as his face cleared the tail of the shirt.

Lacey had brought the sweater up over her head, but her face was still hidden.

Cole stared at the pale pink corset that cupped her breasts and accentuated her waist and hips. With her skirt still on, she looked like a saloon girl from the old west.

As she pulled the sweater free, she took a breath and her areolas peeked above their confines.

He swallowed hard.

"Are you admiring my new corset?" She smiled slyly, the vixen.

He shook his head as he traced a finger along the top edge of the satiny lingerie. "No, I'm admiring this." He pushed his finger inside the cup and flicked at the hard nipple beneath."

"But you like it, right?"

"I think it might require a closer inspection." He used his other hand to burrow beneath her other cup and lift the breast above the soft satin so the corset held it up for him to view her rosy tip. "Hmm, I'm liking it more and more." He performed the same readjustment on her other breast then stood back. "Now that's perfect." He stared at her hard nipples held aloft. "I really like it."

"I'm glad." Her lips formed a seductive pout. "But I lost the bet."

He reached out one hand and brushed his fingertips across her hard nipples. "Yes, you did."

Her chest rose as she sucked in a breath at his touch.

He loved how responsive she was. "I think it's time you took off your skirt so I can decide exactly what position I want you in."

She cocked her head. "And that must be determined by what I'm wearing underneath my skirt?"

He nodded. His soon-to-be wife never failed to surprise him when they crawled into bed at night. Her love of lingerie had him anticipating their alone time even during dinner. He was definitely the beneficiary of that little fetish. It didn't take much to get Lacey hot, but in the house, she had to keep quiet when they made love, and that took something away from the experience for her. Tonight, she could let go completely with no one the wiser.

Lacey untied the bow at her waist and pushed the skirt down to the barn floor before stepping out of it.

He was too distracted by the movement of her breasts at first, to understand her smile.

"So what position would you like?" Her voice was teasing, a sound he hadn't heard in over a month.

This had definitely been needed. He lowered his gaze and raised his brows. "I can't decide until you take off that damn slip too."

She giggled, another sound he hadn't heard in a while. He needed to do something about that. The stress of building a house, working, caring for the horses with so much family around was too stressful for the only-child Lacey.

As she shimmied out of her slip, his jaw dropped and his cock hardened.

Also by Lexi Post

Contemporary Cowboy Romance

Cowboys Never Fold (Poker Flat Series: Book 1)

Cowboy's Match (Poker Flat Series: Book 2)

Cowboy's Best Shot (Poker Flat Series: Book 3)

Cowboy's Break (Poker Flat Series: Book 4)

Wedding at Poker Flat (Poker Flat Series: Book 5)

Christmas with Angel (Poker Flat Series Book 2.5, Last Chance Series: Book 1)

Trace's Trouble (Last Chance Series: Book 2)

Fletcher's Flame (Last Chance Series: Book 3)

Logan's Luck (Last Chance Series: Book 4)

Dillon's Dare (Last Chance Series: Book 5)

Riley's Rescue (Last Chance Series: Book 6) *Coming Soon*

Aloha Cowboy (Island Cowboy Series: Book 1)

Military Romance

When Love Chimes (Broken Valor Series: Book 1)
Poisoned Honor (Broken Valor Series: Book 2)

Paranormal Romance

Masque
Passion's Poison
Passion of Sleepy Hollow
Heart of Frankenstein

Pleasures of Christmas Past (A Christmas Carol Series: Book 1)
Desires of Christmas Present (A Christmas Carol Series: Book 2)
Temptations of Christmas Future (A Christmas Carol: Book 3)
One of A Kind Christmas (A Christmas Carol Series: Book 4)
Coming 2018

On Highland Time (Time Weavers, Inc. Book 1)

Sci-fi Romance

Cruise into Eden (The Eden Series: Book 1)
Unexpected Eden (The Eden Series: Book 2)
Eden Discovered (The Eden Series: Book 3)
Eden Revealed (The Eden Series: Book 4)
Avenging Eden (The Eden Series: Book 5)
Beast of Eden (Eden Series: Book 6) *Coming 2019*

About Lexi Post

Lexi Post is a New York Times and USA Today best-selling author of romance inspired by the classics. She spent years in higher education taking and teaching courses about the classical literature she loved. From Edgar Allan Poe's short story "The Masque of the Red Death" to Tolstoy's *War and Peace*, she's read, studied, and taught wonderful classics.

But Lexi's first love is romance novels. In an effort to marry her two first loves, she started writing romance inspired by the classics and found she loved it. From hot paranormals to sizzling cowboys to hunks from out of this world, Lexi provides a sensuous experience with a "whole lotta story."

Lexi is living her own happily ever after with her husband and her cat in Florida. She makes her own ice cream every weekend, loves bright colors, and you will never see her without a hat.

www.lexipostbooks.com

www.ingramcontent.com/pod-product-compliance
Lightning Source LLC
Chambersburg PA
CBHW070630170726
48291CB00003B/951